ALL THE RAGE IN TEXAS

An Al Quinn Novel

RUSS HALL

All the Rage in Texas
An Al Quinn© Novel
Red Adept Publishing, LLC
104 Bugenfield Court
Garner, NC 27529
https://RedAdeptPublishing.com/

---

1. http://StreetlightGraphics.com

Chapter One

Bonnie looked to the left. *Clear enough.* Then she glanced back at Little Al, who was almost two years old and tucked safely in his booster seat in the right rear of the back seat, where she could keep an eye on him when she had the chance. He clutched a soft green stuffed toy dinosaur.

She had slowed on the ramp and picked up speed as she eased into the empty right lane, heading home, which was still a half hour away. In the seconds she'd been looking back at her child, a black pickup, a Ford F-150 or Dodge Ram, had shot around to the right of an SUV in the fast lane and was barreling directly toward Bonnie's truck.

Since the car in the fast lane was going more than the speed limit, Bonnie didn't dare pull in front of it, cutting it off. Instead, she slammed on the brakes as she veered onto the shoulder. Her wheels hit hard in a series of thumping grinds that threw gravel as her truck skidded and slewed to the right.

The black truck roared past in the so-called slow lane, doing at least seventy. The driver was either waving a fist at Bonnie or flipping her off. His truck was moving too fast for her to catch more than a glimpse of the gesture.

Her truck's engine was idling, but her heart was galloping like Paul Revere's horse on steroids. Adrenaline quivers shot up and down her limbs. She whipped her head around to check on Little Al, who was giggling and waving one fist and the dinosaur in the air. The close call had been an amusement park ride for him but not for Bonnie. *Crazy-ass drivers!*

Traffic was thinning out. She waited until there was a long stretch of no cars coming her way on her side of the divided highway, then she eased back into the slow lane, still breathing hard.

She had only gone half a mile when she saw the black truck sitting on the side of the road a dozen or so car lengths ahead of her. Only a week ago, she had read the account of a man who had sprayed window-washing fluid on his windshield just as a BMW was buzzing by on his left. Some of the spray's speckled drops had gotten on the BMW, and the BMW had pulled over. As the other car went by, shots from the BMW's driver-side window hammered into the car.

"My god, that man's shooting at us!" the woman said.

"I'm hit," her husband told her. He had slumped over the steering wheel, and the car rolled off the road to finally come to rest in the ditch. He was dead by the time an ambulance arrived. The BMW was long gone.

From everything Bonnie had experienced and heard about such situations, she was feeling a dark premonition. So instead of driving by and giving the guy a chance to fill the truck with holes, she slowed and pulled onto the side of the road, half a dozen car lengths behind the black truck. Maybe he would drive away.

"Let's just be careful here," she told Little Al. She reached into her purse and took out her Chiefs Special, a snub-nosed Smith & Wesson loaded with .38 Specials. It wasn't the best sort of gun for any kind of distance shooting, but if anyone got close enough, she could turn him into a saltshaker.

Little Al giggled behind her, but she kept her eyes on the truck, waiting.

Years ago, Bonnie's daddy had taken her out into the woods, in the dark as well as by day, and taught her to shoot until he claimed she could harelip a gnat. He'd taught her how to be cautious and how to wait as well.

Traffic had thinned to almost nothing by the time the black truck's door snapped open. A man stormed out and started back toward Bonnie. The dark object in his hand might have been a cell phone, but when he raised that arm and fired a shot at her, Bonnie knew it wasn't.

She had lowered her window. With her left hand, she squeezed off three answering shots.

The man appeared astonished, but his surprise turned to even more rage. He kept coming, firing away. Shots ricocheted in whining screams, and one punched a tennis-ball-size hole in her windshield.

The truck belonged to Al Quinn, so she slid across to reach into the glove box, knowing that either Al's Glock or his SIG Sauer would be in there. She took out the Glock and slid back over to open her door. Using it as a shield, she stood behind it and went into a shooter's stance, the gun in her right hand. *Bam.*

The guy had been running, getting nearer. The shot hit him in his left thigh, where Bonnie had been aiming. He spun and crumpled to the asphalt, his gun spilling from his hand and landing three feet away. The guy shook his head, cussing loudly, and started to pull himself toward the gun.

Bonnie didn't wait. She hopped back into the truck, put it in gear, and roared out and around the black truck.

"Whee!" Little Al said from the back seat.

Traffic in her direction was so light that she could only see a vehicle or two in the distance in her rearview mirror. A couple of cars going in the other direction across the median strip had pulled over and were probably watching.

Though it was against the law to leave the scene of an accident in Texas, especially if anyone needed help, Bonnie ignored that and pressed harder on the gas. At the next exit, she shot down the ramp, took a left beneath the overpass, and kept going until she came to a thick stand of pecan trees along the two-lane road, where she could pull off and tuck the truck away, out of sight.

She glanced back at her child then took out her phone with trembling hands and dialed Al Quinn's number.

He answered within two rings. "What?"

"Someone just aerated your truck in a few places by taking potshots at Little Al and me. It was a road rage incident."

"You okay?"

"Yeah, but the perp took a bullet to one leg."

"I'm surprised. That's all. The coroner is usually the one dealing with your handiwork."

"I just wanted to get his attention," she said.

"I imagine you did that."

"You'd best come this way." She told him where he could find her. "Your truck's not totaled, but it's not perfect neither."

"I'm on my way."

Bonnie put her phone away and, with Al's Glock in her hand, went around to climb into the backseat of the truck to sit beside her child. She held him close while keeping an eye on the road, which she could barely see through leaves and branches.

ON THE WAY TO WHERE Bonnie waited, Fergie slowed her car as they passed two sheriff's department cruisers pulled over on the opposite side of the road.

"You're not going to stop, are you?" Maury asked from the backseat.

"No need," Al said. The blood smear on the road was already turning brown at its edges. The deputies had probably taken photos. But he doubted if they'd taken a sample for a DNA check, although the two deputies he saw were young and might have watched a lot of television. Only fourteen million or so of America's three hundred thirty million people had any DNA on file. But that might not deter some new and gung ho deputy. So many new deputies had joined the department since Al had retired as one of its detectives that he barely knew any of them.

"It's a wonder there isn't a body lying there for them to look over," Maury said.

"You know Bonnie." Fergie glanced back at him. "She put a bullet right where she wanted."

"I'm as surprised as you she just winged the guy, if Little Al was involved," Maury said.

"From what I've seen of her in action," Al said, "so am I."

Fergie kept going until she came to the same exit Bonnie had taken. She turned left, went through the underpass, and didn't slow until she spotted the big stand of pecan trees.

By looking hard, Al could see flickers of white behind the trunks and undergrowth. Al could hardly wait to see the bullet holes in his truck. But Bonnie and Little Al were the priorities of the moment.

Fergie eased off the road and nudged her car's way through the thick green until the truck could be seen.

Maury had the back door open and was running across to the truck even before Fergie came to a stop.

Al hopped out of the front passenger side as soon as Fergie stopped and turned off her engine. Bonnie was hugging Little Al in the truck's backseat while Maury leaned in to hug them both.

"*Tsk. Tsk.*" Al shook his head at the bullet hole through his windshield and a couple more in the driver's-side door.

"There is one thing," Bonnie said. "When I was driving away, I looked back and saw that guy pulling himself across the asphalt to get his gun, so I hit the gas pedal harder and skedaddled out of there pronto."

"And?" Al asked.

"He was looking up, and I think there's a pretty good chance he got your license plate number."

"So you think it's likely we might get company?" Fergie asked. Bonnie nodded.

AS AL PARKED HIS TRUCK at his mechanic's shop, Lenny came over, shaking his head. "*Tsk. Tsk,*" he echoed Al.

"I know. It's not just an oil change this time. I'll see how much my insurance company can handle, and I'm good for the rest myself."

Lenny shook his head again and took the key Al held out to him.

Al pulled out his phone to call the sheriff's department, where he had been a detective for thirty years.

When he was patched through to Victor Kahlon, the detective who had taken Al's place, Al explained the situation.

"I'm glad you called, Al. I heard about some shooting out on that highway. I'm glad you didn't make us piece things together. Both vehicles fled the scene. Now we know one participant in the fracas. Since Bonnie was driving your truck, I'm surprised the other guy lived."

"Especially since her son was in the backseat," Al said. "But she's trying to be less hair-trigger these days and more compassionate toward her fellow man, the way she tells it. But I imagine she was seeing bright red. We're heading back to my place now. Send someone by if you want a statement."

"I'll come myself. Sheriff Clayton's been wanting to do something about road rage incidents. We had another fatality just last week."

"I heard about that. Guy was found face down and not moving in a private driveway his car was blocking."

"We're looking into causes, but road rage is our top hunch for now," Victor said.

"I heard that Austin and the Texas Department of Public Safety are having powwows on the same thing."

"The numbers are sure up on our roads as well as in Austin. Sheriff Clayton would like to do something preventative instead of just landing on the perps like a ton of bricks."

"Short of handing out Valium or Xanax to stressed-out drivers, I don't know what he plans to do about it."

"I don't either, Al. But I'm sure he and I will have a conversation about it. I'll see you at your house in a bit."

Al waved to Lenny and got in the front passenger seat of Fergie's car. Maury and Bonnie were crowded into the backseat, with Little Al's booster seat fastened down between them.

Al thought of all the road rage incidents he'd covered when he was a detective, and he'd been involved only because a fatality needed investigation.

He understood rage, from flash anger to burning, simmering hate, as he'd been no stranger to those emotions himself. Al glanced back at Maury, who flashed him a smile before bending back down to entertain Little Al by making faces at him.

Too readily, Al could recall the time when he had come home early and caught Maury with Al's first wife, Abbie. Maury had been the best man at their wedding and had apparently set out to prove it. Al had divorced Abbie and stayed away from Maury, not speaking to him for twenty years, for he feared he would have killed him. He had felt both the initial explosive rage and the long-simmering hate. But they had worked all that out, and they all lived in the same house, the one where Al had planned to spend his retirement years in solitude.

Look at me now. Married to Fergie, who was the worst high school prom date ever.

They were all silent all the way back to Al's house beside the lake. They'd had a frog-walloper of a rainstorm for a week or so a while back after a couple of months of drought. The roadside woods were bursting with green again and getting thick and concealing, especially around the entrance to his lane.

Fergie went slower than usual, heading down the lane to Al's house on the shore of Lake Travis. Al realized why as they came around a stand of trees and thick brush. A black truck was parked in front of the house.

"Uh-oh." Fergie came to a stop.

"Wait here," Al said. He got out of the car as quietly as he could with his Glock in hand.

Fergie held a hand out to the backseat. Bonnie put her small Chiefs Special into it, and she got out, too, trailing behind Al, who was moving quickly but carefully toward the house. A man was standing at the front door, a belt wrapped tightly around one leg, like a makeshift tourniquet. He pounded on the door and pushed a finger hard on the doorbell.

As Al got closer, he could hear Tanner barking from inside. He wished he could tell the dog not to do that.

The man at the door raised his gun and shot at the door, right toward where Tanner would be on the other side.

Heat and a red haze shot in a wave through Al's head. He had felt flash anger a time or two before and didn't care for it, but it had always given him an enormous amount of energy. He broke into a flat-out run.

The man looked ready to fire again. Al slammed the barrel of his pistol down on the man's wrist and heard a satisfying crack as he broke at least one bone, maybe two. The gun dropped to the ground.

The man spun just as Al slammed into him, knocking him to the ground.

Although the guy was big, Al flipped him onto his back and pinned him to the ground, that red-hot anger giving him the strength of two men. Tanner whined on the other side of the door.

The man glared up at Al, starting to squirm to get free in spite of his badly broken right wrist.

Fergie stepped in close and pressed the barrel of the Chiefs Special hard against the guy's forehead. His eyes crossed as he stared up at the gun.

"Don't make me have to pull this trigger," Fergie said with the firm voice she had used for more than thirty years as an Austin police detective. "I would hate to have to wade through the pile of paperwork. The likes of you aren't worth the bother."

The man stopped squirming, and his eyes fixed on Fergie's face, which was every bit as firm and determined as her voice had been.

"Maury!" Al snarled through clenched teeth.

Maury handed the baby to Bonnie and went to unlock the door. He entered the house then came rushing back out in barely a minute. He held out handcuffs to Al and swung the barrel of the Model 12 Winchester shotgun at the fallen man and jacked a shell into the chamber.

The face of the man on the ground was twisted in pain. But he refused to speak.

That was okay with Al. He grabbed the man's good leg and dragged him across the lawn to the base of a mesquite tree, where a metal pipe with a faucet on its end stuck out of the ground. Al snapped one end of the handcuffs on the man's good wrist and fastened the other end to the pipe tightly enough that it wasn't going to go anywhere. He reached down and yanked the guy's wallet and cell phone out of his pockets.

"Hey," the guy finally said. "You can't do that. You have no search warrant. I have rights."

"Get this guy." Fergie shook her head. She moved closer to him and kept her gun pointed at him while Maury stood on the other side with the barrel of the shotgun pointed at the man's belly.

"We're not cops right now," Al said. "And you have no rights."

He turned and ran to the front door. Inside, Tanner was growling and trying to get outside. The dog stopped as soon as he recognized Al, who reached down and took a close look at the blood on Tanner's back, which was dripping onto the rug. A shot had carved a line that ran across a third of Tanner's back and his rump.

Tanner's tail started wagging, and Al gave him a hug. The dog followed Al as he went to get a blanket. He wrapped Tanner in it and tied the belt of his robe around the dog to apply pressure to slow the bleeding. Then he picked him up and headed out the door.

"I'm off to the vet!" he yelled as he got into Fergie's car. "If that guy so much as twitches, you know what to do."

"Hey, I'm hurt here!" the guy yelled, still with more anger than contrition.

Fergie moved between him and Bonnie, who in spite of holding the baby was moving in to kick the guy.

When Al was halfway up the drive, a beige truck came screeching in. One of the sheriff's department's silver Chevy Tahoe cruisers was right behind the truck. As the lead truck barreled toward him, Al slowed. The driver's window rolled down.

"Where are you off to?" Victor Kahlon asked.

Al glanced back at the deputy in the following silver SUV. He was too young for Al to know him, but Al was glad to see that Victor had brought backup.

"Taking Tanner to the vet. That dumbass shot him through the front door." Al held out the guy's wallet and cell phone to Victor. "You can see who he is and who he called at the DMV to get my address. You'd best get back there before Bonnie gets to the guy. He's the one who shot at her and her child."

Before Victor could respond, Al hit the gas and took off toward the end of his drive. He was soon heading for his vet's office at a good bit above the posted speed limit.

On the way, he broke a personal rule and made a cell phone call to the vet so she would be ready and waiting. Once he'd done that, he put away the phone and went a little faster.

A quick glance at Tanner showed the dog was bleeding through the blanket. His head stuck out one end of the cloth, which was rolled around him, making him look like a burrito. His face was calm, and his eyes were fixed on Al. He obviously trusted his human.

Tanner had been a senior Australian shepherd in a rescue center. He had been two days away from being euthanized when Al spotted him and took him home. Al had never regretted the decision for a moment. The dog's calm helped him.

Though Al was no stranger to anger, he had, through the years, come to deal with it better. When a car pulled out into traffic ahead of him, causing him to slow, he supposed the driver had been sitting there for a longish spell and had finally snapped and pushed out into traffic that hadn't seemed to let up. Al tried to think from the other person's perspective, to understand, and to forgive. He suspected, though, that not everyone else had come to that state of comprehension, especially that jasper back there on the ground who was just a tick away from being kicked in the crotch by Bonnie. That fellow wasn't alone in a world fueled by rage. There were way too many others in an increasingly crowded landscape, all of them like so many ticking time bombs.

Tanner was still staring at him, his face full of trust and patience.

"You were only barking to defend the house," Al said. "You're no biter. I don't know how you'd fare in a world of humans. Some of them are self-absorbed jerks, nothing to be proud of at all. It's gotten to be a pretty edgy place we live in nowadays."

He pulled into the vet's parking lot, scooped up Tanner, blanket and all, and headed inside.

Chapter Two

Fergie moved closer to the man on the ground, keeping her body between him and Bonnie, who was edging around toward him, even though she held Little Al. Maury kept his shotgun pointed down at the guy, who tugged at the wrist handcuffed to the pipe.

"Don't let Bonnie near him," Fergie said to Maury. "She's still a touch riled up."

Maury nodded. Bonnie had been a nurse and might have tried to help anyone else who was hurt but not someone who had shot at her and Little Al and who had shot Tanner.

Fergie turned her head to the sound of two vehicles coming up the drive to the house. She recognized Kahlon's truck, and the cruiser following him spoke for itself.

As they pulled up to the end of the lane and got out, an ambulance siren in the distance told them it was heading their way.

"Good." She nodded toward the guy handcuffed to the pipe on the ground. Blood was seeping through his jeans in spite of his makeshift tourniquet, and his right hand hung loosely beside him. "He's going to need that."

"Knowing Bonnie was involved, I feared I might have to skip ahead to the meat wagon," Victor said.

Bonnie was still trying to edge around Maury to get to the guy.

The uniformed deputy glanced at Victor, asking without words if he needed to hold Bonnie back.

Victor shook his head. Maury had experience when it came to herding her, and he was getting the job done.

"We'll be glad for you to take this dirtbag off our hands," Fergie said.

"Y'all think you're gooder'n me, don't ya." The guy glared up at Fergie then Bonnie.

Victor glanced at Fergie.

She said, "Ah, you send the lad to Eton and Oxford, and this is the sort of mouth gargle you get. What a shame."

"What's that skinny ol' string bean mean?" the man asked Victor.

"I think she was poking a little fun at you," Victor said.

"You'd best remember one word, and that's payback." His eyes narrowed and were nearly throwing sparks. Then he glanced at his broken wrist, which was starting to swell. He didn't look sad. He looked angry. "And oh hey. They stole my wallet and phone. I got rights here."

Victor held them up. "It was due cause, and no one stole anything, Randolph Baker Ketchum."

"Give me them back."

"You're going to the hospital then to a cell. These will be waiting for you."

"I got friends. Payback. Remember that," he said, spraying spit.

"Really? You're talking revenge while being arrested?" Victor Kahlon shook his head.

"Arrested? They're the ones done harm to me. Just look at me!" Ketchum shouted.

The ambulance's siren had gotten louder, and its lights were flashing as the yellow-and-blue truck pulled up and stopped. Two EMS workers in blue jumped out and came running with their carry kits.

Victor leaned closer. "A witness driving a company van with a dash camera with audio caught the whole incident. It was one vile bit of rage, which you compounded by finding out where these people lived and coming after them in their home."

"No way. No way. It's all them. They started it. You just wait until I get me a lawyer."

"A deputy is also picking up your asshole buddy Biff Groton at the DMV right now, the one you called. Maybe you'll share a cell."

One of the EMS workers looked up at Victor and frowned. He was trying to get a splint on Ketchum's wrist and might have thought the detective was winding up the patient.

Victor and Fergie stepped back, letting the emergency crew do their thing. The guy mumbled and moaned, acting like he was the victim.

"It's that way with some of these road ragers." Victor shook his head. "They get to spouting off and start believing their own BS, that they were the ones being wronged. It's lucky we have a bit of film on this one. His version of the story doesn't hold a thimble of water."

Maury put the shotgun inside the front door of the house and moved closer to Bonnie and their baby. "Is this sort of thing on the upswing?"

"Oh my gosh, yes." Victor turned to him. "Our numbers are the highest ever, and Austin even has a new task force to deal with road rage. I blame it a little on some of the political divisiveness, increased stress about work and health, and the population in particular."

"The population?" Maury reached out to give Bonnie a break from holding the baby.

"You ever hear about Malthus?" Victor asked.

"Does he live around here?" Bonnie squinted at him.

"No. Victor's talking about some English dude from about two hundred and fifty years ago," Fergie said.

"Anyway," Victor said, "his Malthusian theory involved worrying that the population was growing too fast. Personally, I think he was onto something. Check any reference to the population when you were born then when you graduated from high school and about every twenty years or so after that. The population has been doubling at a horrific pace, and it seems they all own cars, and half of them are mightily ticked off about one thing or another."

The EMS crew signaled to Victor that they needed him to unlock the handcuff holding Ketchum's good wrist to the water pipe. As soon as he was free, they slid him onto a stretcher. Victor clicked the other end of the handcuffs to the steel side of it. Then the two EMS workers popped Ketchum into the back of the ambulance like a loaf of bread going into an oven. He was still muttering and mumbling as the doors closed.

"See you at the hospital," Victor told the crew.

He waved his right forefinger in a circle in the air and pointed at the cruiser. The uniformed deputy got in and started backing up the drive.

"Now I just need to get a statement from Bonnie, and I'll be on my way," Victor said. "Like as not, there's been another such incident while I've been tending to this one."

AL GLANCED OVER AT Tanner, who was sprawled across the front passenger seat of Fergie's car. White gauze and tape covered the furrow where the vet had stitched together the bullet's grazing path. The vet tech had trimmed away some of Tanner's fur before the vet made like Betsy Ross on the dog's back.

"Don't worry, Tanner. You can get by with a comb-over until your fur grows back. At least you don't have to wear a cone of shame."

Tanner looked up at Al, his mouth open and his tongue hanging out, which was nearly a smile. Al had been looking forward to Tanner rushing toward them with his tail wagging as vigorously as possible when they got home. But that hothead Ketchum had thrown a spanner into that cozy scene.

Al caught a whiff now and again of the tape, gauze, and some sort of antiseptic the vet had used. *Give it to dogs. They bounce back better than humans.*

He was glad the dog was okay, and Tanner seemed to have rolled well with the adventure. Al hadn't thought a lot about what a mystical thing love for a pet was. But he had bursts of insight, like when seeing his dog, with that patch of white fur on his snout, looking up at him and giving his tail a brave half wag.

"At least the guy who did this to you is going to be safely behind bars soon and can't try to hurt you again."

SHIRLEY ANN BARRISTER looked down at a smudge on her white uniform then moved quickly past the door to Mr. Brinkly's room. He was likely to ask for yet another sponge bath, and she was in no mood for his shenanigans. She was minutes away from the end of her twelve-hour shift and felt tired to her bones. Her feet were like two anvils. As soon as she got home, she was going to kick off her shoes and pour herself a nice chilled glass of Relax Riesling, perfect in name, taste, and effect.

In walked Janey Pond, the head nurse of the next shift, who was always early. She was carrying a foil-covered paper plate of her to-die-for cookies. The hospital's well-being program had been seeking to cut down on people bringing cookies, donuts, brownies, or chocolates to their colleagues. *But bless Janey for defying them.*

Then Shirley Ann caught a glimpse of Janey's face. Her eyes were open wide, and the skin of her cheeks was pulled as tight as rictus and had turned pale enough to make her whitish-gray hair look dark. Shirley Ann had been so fixed on the plate of cookies that she'd missed the doctor pressed close behind Janey. *No. That's no doctor.* Shirley Ann knew all the doctors on the floor. The guy behind the surgical mask was a stranger, an unwanted one, with determined, intense eyes and perhaps with a gun pointed at Janey's back.

Removing all doubt, the man held his gun hand out around Janey and waved them both toward a room down the hall, where a sheriff's deputy sat on a chair in the hallway. He was reading a *Reader's Digest* but dropped it to the floor as the three of them came up to him. The man in the mask pointed his gun at the deputy's face. So he rose and let the man take his sidearm as he herded all three of them into the room where Mr. Ketchum lay with his good arm handcuffed to the bed.

"Biff," Ketchum said.

"No names," Biff said though a tad too late.

The deputy was a tall, thin redheaded young man with freckles and the face of someone barely out of his teens. A red flush covered both cheeks, and he looked as frightened as Shirley Ann felt. Perhaps he was pondering how the situation would affect his career.

Shirley Ann debated whether she should scream. But that might get them shot. Also, she wasn't sure she *could* scream. Her lungs felt like they'd crowded up into her throat.

Moving soundlessly, Biff undid the handcuff from Ketchum's wrist and fastened it to the deputy's wrist.

Ketchum would have been unable to use crutches, so he held the deputy's gun on them while Biff went out and came back with a wheelchair. Before they went out the door, Biff ripped the cords of both phones in the room out of the wall and tossed the phones onto the floor. Then they were out the door.

"Any idea how we can call for security?" The deputy was looking down at the phones, which lay in a tangle.

"I suggest we wait a minute to give them time to get in the elevator," Janey said, "then we start screaming like crazy."

"Would you mind terribly much if I had one of your cookies in the meantime?" Shirley Ann asked in a voice that quivered almost out of control.

Chapter Three

As Al drove Fergie's car down the woods-lined last stretch of drive to his house, he saw Victor Kahlon's truck parked out front.

"Hold onto your whiskers, Tanner." Al glanced down at his bandaged dog as he pulled up behind Victor's truck. "This doesn't bode well—probably bad news of some sort or other."

No one was outside, so Al hefted Tanner down to the ground and let him follow as he walked to the front door and went inside.

"There he is!" Maury yelled. "Our hero dog, Tanner, who took a bullet while defending our home."

As Al went through the foyer, he noticed that the blood had been cleaned up from the floor. Someone, probably Bonnie, had done some heavy-duty cleaning.

Victor Kahlon sat at the dining table with a mug of coffee in front of him. Beside him, looming as large as John Wayne, sat Sheriff Clayton. His hair was a bit whiter than the last time Al had seen him, but he still looked as fit as he was big. His face always seemed like it had been chiseled out of stubborn rock, and the last few years had etched the lines even deeper. He was older than Al yet had not retired, preferring to run his department as a tight, efficient ship.

Maury stood up to make room for Al at the table. Fergie sat across from the detective and the sheriff. She raised her mug and pointed at it. Al nodded, so Fergie rose to get him a mug of coffee.

Bonnie came up from the basement and held a finger to her lips. "Take it easy, everyone. I just got Little Al down for a nap. He's had a helluva day."

"What brings you out here?" Al sat and looked across the table at Clayton. "I didn't know you made house calls anymore. In fact, I can't remember the last time you left your office."

"It's been over three years," Clayton said, "if you're keeping track."

"So again, what brings you here?"

"You'd best have a sip of coffee first." Clayton nodded to the mug Fergie was holding out to Al.

While Al took accepted the coffee, Clayton bent to pet Tanner, who had gone over to him. He petted the parts of the dog not covered by white tape and gauze. "Looks like you've been to the wars," he said.

"He sure took one for the team," Bonnie said. "I'm glad that jasper is locked up. I hope you threw away the key."

"That's what I came to talk to you all about," Clayton said, his voice deepening. It was already like gravel being unloaded from a steel truck, so when it went lower, it became even more ominous. He turned to Victor. "You'd better fill them in."

"The thing is—" Victor's face took on a sheepish expression. "Ketchum got away. One of his pals, Biff Groton, we're pretty sure, sprang him free from the hospital, where a single rookie deputy was watching him while he was resting from getting his bullet wound patched and having surgery to set the bones in his arm. He was moments away from being whisked off to jail. Instead, he's in the wind."

Al caught Fergie's raised eyebrow. "You checked where these guys live?" he asked.

"Biff's place was a one-room dive that looked like he never cleaned it. He had cleared out his possessions, mostly guns, and left a mess the landlord is still ranting about. In addition to saying goodbye to his deposit, Biff's job at the DMV is history, and he'll probably be skipping on the bail he posted earlier. So all in all, a trifecta-of-burned-bridges sort of day for him."

"And Ketchum's place?"

"Biff must have popped in to Ketchum's single-wide earlier and picked up his extra ammo and guns to add to his own armory. That's short of what was in Ketchum's truck, which we impounded. I doubt that made him any more cheerful. Ketchum was three months late on his payments for the trailer, and his clearing out was one step ahead of a repo man."

"A couple of fine citizens," Fergie said. "They can just pick up like that and leave their lives behind?"

"Seems so," Victor said. "Ketchum lost his job a month ago. He worked as an auto mechanic but got caught stealing tools and selling them, not red-handed, but everything pointed to him. So he was pretty sore about getting canned, enough that he talked about coming back and torching the place. Before he could add arson to his resume, the shop put in a new security system that would have put him away. That just made him madder. By lying on his resume, he somehow managed to get a job as a customer service rep at a sporting goods store. He was let go from that for punching a customer on the morning of the day he and Bonnie crossed paths. So he's been going around with a chip on his shoulder the size of the Capitol Building."

Clayton shook his head. "That's not all," he rumbled.

Victor started to drink from his mug, found it empty, and waved Fergie back to her seat when she rose to give him a refill. "As you know, the guy at the DMV who gave him your address is Ketchum's pal Biff Groton. We brought him in based on information we found on Ketchum's phone. We had just enough to hold him for a Privacy Act violation by a DMV employee, which is a misdemeanor charge, and we tried to throw a scare into him about a five-thousand-dollar fine, but he clammed up on us. We had to let him out on bail."

"I sense we're easing up to the juicy part of the story," Al said.

Victor nodded. "So like I said, we're pretty sure it was Biff Groton who showed up at the hospital before we could transfer Ketchum to jail. He took the weapon away from the lone rookie deputy we had watching Ketchum's room until the transfer could be made. He was literally going out one door with Ketchum while our unit was pulling up to another door to transport Ketchum to jail. If we get our hands on Biff this time, I'm pretty sure we can land charges on him like a ton of bricks. But…"

"I'll bet this really gets better now," Fergie said.

"Yeah. Ketchum and Biff Groton are in the wind all right. But there are also three more of them."

"They're a gang?"

"A bunch of like-minded men, you could say, who hung out together at a shooting range out on the edge of the county." Victor appeared to change his mind about the coffee and got up to take his mug to the pot on the stove and refill it. "Picture this. They met one another at a court-appointed anger-management class. Each had been guilty of spousal abuse, and all are divorced now—a common cause or pattern. The guy who runs the shooting range, Heck Marmon, says they call themselves the RKs."

"Have you reached out to the other three members in your effort to round up Ketchum and Groton?" Al asked.

"Yep, and here's the chilling part. They've all picked up and skedaddled as well."

"You think Ketchum is their leader and they're planning something like that payback he was talking about?"

Victor nodded. "More like a jihad, if these guys are the sort I think they are."

Al glanced at Fergie at the same second she looked at him. She shook her head. He thought, *So much for those quiet years of retirement, fishing, and kicking back, living the good life.*

Maury had moved closer to Bonnie. They both looked at Al, who turned to the sheriff.

"The real sixty-four-thousand-dollar question is why you're here personally. You'll notice that this is at least the third time I've asked the question."

"Duly noted. I'll let Victor set up what I have to say."

"We had a tactical meeting to discuss what we could do about the growing road rage problem."

"Short of throwing a bucket of cold water on anyone who starts to look miffed in traffic?" Bonnie asked.

"Yeah, short of that." Victor frowned at her. "We've tried public service messages, but the ones really needing to think more about it aren't usually good listeners. The public knows there's a problem. In 2021, for instance, there were forty-four people per month killed or wounded in road rage incidents. Texas had five hundred twenty-two road rage shootings in 2021, and well over half of all highway fatalities were caused by road rage. One suggestion was to have civilians enlisted to watch for such events and report them. But there were several things wrong with that."

"We have deputies on the road in greater numbers than ever," Clayton rumbled, "and the one thing we want to avoid above all others is encouraging vigilantism of any kind. We also have to avoid anything that could remotely be construed as entrapment."

"Long story short..." Victor started.

"Too late," Al said.

"Anyway, the consensus of opinion was that we needed to catch as many as we could of those causing these road rage incidents and have a fair public trial where the example is made to show we're serious about shutting down this sort of thing. With what we had, Ketchum looked like he was going to fit nicely into that sort of handling. We had a pretty good case against him."

"But now he's as gone as the dodo," Bonnie said.

Victor glared at her.

"I don't suppose he's going to stay missing for long," Clayton said.

Al caught something in the sheriff's tone. "You don't think...?"

"Let's have Victor tell you a bit more about these RKs."

Victor gave a quick shrug as if not too eager. "Well, we know there are at least five of them and that Ketchum seems to be the alpha dog among them. Since tipping off Ketchum, Boudreaux 'Biff' Groton hasn't called the DMV to see if he still has a job, which is just as well, since they intend to fire him. And they're behind the misdemeanor charge against him for sharing private information."

"I'll bet the others are a lively bunch of coconuts as well," Bonnie said.

"You're not wrong. Kale Durant is the smooth talker and good looker of them but with no steady job, although he always seems to have money. He's had three wives, none of whom want any more to do with him. Like so many con men or scammers, he projects what some describe as an 'illusion of innocence.' I say don't believe it, not for a second. Cable Early is one of those fellows who makes knives and sells them along the roadside. Folks who know him like to say he was born a couple hundred years too late, that he could have thrived in the hunter, survival days of Daniel Boone or any other number of mountain men or such. He was once caught by Fish and Wildlife for trying to sell venison, white-tailed deer, out of season. He didn't have a license, and they've labeled him a poacher. Eugene 'Buff' Lohmann—the Buff is short for buffalo—is bigger than almost any pro offensive lineman and was a bouncer who got too enthusiastic at a kicker bar and nearly broke some cowboy in half. The club is getting sued and wants nothing to do with Buff, who they fired."

"If this Buff is so big, why isn't he the alpha one of them?" Maury asked.

"That says more about Ketchum than Buff," Victor said. "They all have military experience, as well, though far from distinguished."

"So five guys with badly checkered pasts that give them a common cause," Fergie said.

Victor nodded. "We're talking about a bunch of guys so steeped in the poison of their beliefs that their goal in life is to violently defend their right to hate and be angry."

"That's where your bunch comes in, Al," Clayton said.

"I'll bet I'm not going to like this part." Al glanced at Fergie.

"I doubt you will." Clayton cleared his throat. "We have absolutely no idea where these guys are holed up, if they're even together. But we suspect they are. The telling aspect of them is defined by Ketchum. Not only did he get enraged enough to shoot at Bonnie, but he stayed mad and came to your house. A sustained rage suggests they'll be prone to revenge, something Ketchum has already declared. There's every chance he views this as some sort of Hatfield-McCoy thing."

"I don't want to be used as the cheese in a trap."

"I can't see that you have much choice," Victor said. "These guys are probably going to come at you all like hornets out of a kicked nest."

"The thing is," Clayton said, "we need them alive so they can go through the court system—be an example and a deterrent so some hotheads will think twice when the heat on the road overtakes them."

"If they come, they won't be pulling any punches," Al said.

"But I'd like your bunch to do so, if at all possible," Clayton said, "especially Annie Bonnie Oakley there. We want these guys alive. I know it's a lot to ask."

"You might as well ask for the moon." Maury was looking at Bonnie.

"We'll do what we can," Al said. "But I'm not promising anything. If these guys threaten our lives, or even that of our dog, they might be headed for a bad day at the box office. So I know what you want, what would be convenient, but if you want these five hard cases wrapped up with a bow, I really can't promise you a thing."

"I understand," Clayton said. "All I can ask is that you try."

AL WOKE WHEN HE HEARD Tanner stirring. The dog needed to go outside. Perhaps because of the trauma of the day, Tanner hadn't settled into one of his beds but had curled up at the foot of theirs.

Al touched Fergie's shoulder without waking her. The luminous dial on his watch showed it was one-thirty in the morning. The white of Tanner's bandages glowed in the moonlight as he moved about in the room.

He pulled on his jeans and put his bare feet into his boots. Nobody else in the house was stirring, though he knew Maury, Bonnie, and the baby were on the floor below.

When he opened the front door, half a dozen deer rose from where they'd been curled up on his front lawn. He was glad he'd slipped the leash on Tanner, even if the dog wasn't disposed to worrying the deer that liked to stay close to Al's house.

The moon was full and round. Tanner left a territory-marking pee mail or two and did some more serious business on the spot where Ketchum had been handcuffed to the water pipe earlier, perhaps making a statement, since he could surely detect a scent.

The deer were settling back into their spots as Al walked the dog up the lane a ways toward the road until he could catch the glimmer of one of the silver sheriff's department SUVs tucked into the woods beside the lane. Soft lights inside the cruiser hinted that the deputy might be listening to music or reading. Al turned Tanner around, and they headed back for the house.

Anyone wanting to threaten Al's house could always come across the water, since he lived right on the shore of Lake Travis. He imagined Clayton had arranged for one of the department boats to swing past now and then.

So it's like that.

Well, he shouldn't complain. But he said to Tanner, "How does it feel to be like that bit of cheese in a trap waiting for a mouse I mentioned earlier?"

Chapter Four

"They won't be expecting this. Sly genius in a nutshell's what this is." R. B. Ketchum sat in the passenger seat of the pickup Kale Durant had driven to the next county, where a National Guard armory was situated right behind a barracks and the recruitment office. All the buildings were empty or nearly as empty as they ever got.

The sky was black and the moon waning gibbous, beginning to get smaller after the full moon, still providing enough light for Cable Early to slip outside the truck to scout ahead for any security patrols they hadn't foreseen. Within feet of where they were parked, his shape grew dimmer then disappeared.

"That ol' Cable plain moves like some coon-ass Injun," Ketchum muttered. He had a Ruger .357 tucked into his belt at the front, where he could get at it with his left hand, and had gone through half a box of ammo to make sure he could still shoot as a southpaw. But if all went well, he wouldn't need to get out of the truck. His left leg was far from ready for any serious walking about anyway.

While the armory was supposed to be only unlockable from a terminal inside the barracks, Biff Groton knew they could also get inside by picking a Master level lock, a skill he possessed. Buff Lohmann, beside Biff in the backseat of the truck, held bolt cutters, though they hoped not to need them.

Kale Durant asked, "When this is over, then what?"

"They'll think Mexico. Instead, we head out west, where hardly anyone lives and where we can slip off the grid for as long as we want."

"You mean where men are men and the sheep are nervous?" Biff asked.

"More likely where men are men and so are the women," Kale said.

"We can't just go there now?" Buff asked in a voice so low Ketchum barely heard him.

"Right now, we have unfinished business," he said, glancing back to the lump that was Buff. "Everyone talks about mindless violence. We're about to school them 'bout mindful violence. Take my truck and two of my best guns, will they."

Kale nodded.

He and Cable Early planned to go in while Buff Lohmann stood guard. Ketchum was already picturing his crew with rocket launchers, grenades, and howitzers. They had pistols, rifles, and shotguns. What he craved was something a little harder hitting. All of them had military experience, if they put aside three dishonorable discharges and one faked injury.

When Cable Early had been scouting that Quinn guy's house, he'd tumbled to the sheriff's department stakeout as well as a boat patrol that went by every two hours at night. That was flimsy protection, at best, and couldn't last long.

Suddenly, Cable's head popped up right outside Ketchum's window. If he noticed that he'd given Ketchum a start, he didn't let on. He nodded toward the backseat.

"You guys are up now," Ketchum said. "In and out. Pronto."

KALE STAYED RIGHT BEHIND Cable, with Buff behind him and Biff pulling up the rear. *Biff and Buff. How did that even happen?* He stepped carefully where leaf litter had accumulated and could rustle.

The night was almost black except for an occasional glitter of stars when the cloud cover cleared, sometimes letting the moon show through. Beams of light trickled through the foliage of the woods from the security lights around the buildings.

Ketchum had been right about Cable. He made less noise than a soft wind when he moved.

Buff, on the other hand, was trying to move soundlessly but failing. His steps were like those of his namesake, a buffalo.

Kale was trying to estimate how much farther they had to go. They had to be about halfway to the chain-link fence, the reason Buff was carrying the bolt cutters.

Cable held up a hand and stopped. Kale nearly ran into him.

Just enough light filtering through the trees allowed Kale to make out a dim figure standing ahead of them. It was Val Hanson, Kale's inside connection. He'd met him a while back in a bar and had let Val come to his own conclusions about Kale's preferences. When the others asked if he'd had to consummate the friendship, he'd told them he didn't consummate his relationships with half the females he strung along and took advantage of. He was a born user, and it was hardly his fault if there were so many people in the world eager to be used.

Kale stepped around Cable and moved closer to Val. "What are you doing out here? I thought you were just going to help us get in."

"There's more going on inside right now than I expected. I thought you weren't going to make your try for another week or two."

"Our timetable moved up."

Val waved a hand at two long boxes on the ground beside him. "I had the devil's own time dragging these out here. They're heavier than I thought. Your man there said to leave them on the ground and wait on you."

"Are you going to be able to get any more?"

"No way, man. Like I said, it's busy inside, and I shouldn't have even tried to get these out. Who knows if they'll miss them right away."

As if in answer, sirens started up at the armory, and several more lights turned on, making the woods brighter, even as far away as they were.

"Oh my heavens. I may be busted. You'd best get out of here."

"Well, thanks." Kale sighed.

Buff had been moving closer, as if to look down at the two boxes. He reached to grab Val's head and gave it a quick twist. Val crumpled to the ground like a loose bag of sand. Then Buff picked up one of the boxes.

Kale shook his head and bent to get the other. They all headed back toward the truck to make a quick departure. It was an armory, so Kale doubted there would be dogs. He didn't even like to think about running through the dense growth with dogs on their heels.

None of them spoke as they broke into a near run. Buff's formerly loud steps sounded like a stampede. They hadn't gotten nearly as much as they'd wanted—as much as Ketchum thought they needed—and would probably have to move on to plan B. Kale would rather they didn't have to do that, since it didn't bode well for their friend Heck Marmon. But into each life some rain must fall.

Chapter Five

Bonnie came out of the upstairs master bedroom carrying Al's 30-06. She'd gotten it out of the gun safe in Al and Fergie's room.

Al and Fergie stood side by side on the second level, looking out the windows by the porch at the stretch of Lake Travis. Each of them held a mug in one hand. It always seemed a little odd to Bonnie to see Fergie standing half a foot taller than Al.

"It's an awful thing when the house you feel comfortable in doesn't feel safe anymore," Fergie said, "and someone is making it that way, someone who doesn't have to but does so out of raw malice. Out of their own festering bile."

Al caught a glimpse of Bonnie going by, carrying his rifle. "You going out for a quick look around again? This is the third night in a row this week."

"Yep. I got Little Al tucked in, and Maury's keeping an eye on him, probably asleep himself by now. I got a restless itch to know what's goin' on."

"Want either or both of us along?" Fergie asked.

"Nope. I kinda enjoy tromping around out there on my own, bein' as quiet as a field mouse in slippers. The wind talks to me, and I can have a good look about."

Tanner, who had been curled up on his bed in a corner of the room, got up slowly and with creaky steps caused by the stiffening wraps around his patched wound came over to Bonnie. Normally, he would be ready to charge out the door with her to terrorize the villagers. But he could barely move.

She reached down to pet his head. "It's brave of you to ask, but you can't come along, old fella. You're still on the mend."

Al went over to hold the dog gently and keep him from going along on the outing.

As Bonnie slipped out the front door and closed it behind her, she kept the little SureFire high-intensity flashlight in her pocket. Her pappy had taught her to work on her night eyes and not lean on lights unless she absolutely had to.

Bonnie raised the rifle and looked through the scope then swung it across a patch of lane and woods ahead. She could see pretty well. As she lowered it, she worked the bolt and slid a round of ammo into the chamber.

The moon was doing that thing where a crescent rocked on the bottom and the outline of the rest shone above it. The stars were bright. The Little Dipper and the rest were all doing their jobs. She couldn't imagine living in the city, where all the lights kept anyone from seeing and enjoying the stars each night.

Bonnie started up slowly and carefully on the lane at first and soon slipped into the woods, where she would be darn near invisible to anyone ahead of her.

In the distance, a couple of coyotes started to kick up the usual fuss with their howling, then a chorus of tiny howls joined in as the litter got all worked up.

A lizard made a clatter as it scampered through dry leaves, and above her, an owl seemed to be clearing its throat. Her senses were heightened to the point that she caught every little thing, each nuance as she slipped through the woods in the dark of night.

Bonnie could smell the musky black soil and rotting leaves and imagined worms tunneling below and insects scurrying and nibbling. But there was the looming chance she might need to use her gun. That sent a ripple of readiness through her.

She loved those times, never felt more alive than when she was out on her own and there was some danger, some risk.

Ahead, the glimmer of silver showed where the sheriff's department SUV was nestled in a stand of mountain cedar beside the lane. She raised the scope again in time to see the deputy climb out the driver's door and head for a nearby tree. Not caring to see what he had in mind, she swung the scope away. As she did, she picked up on a flutter of movement up the lane. Just as she started to make out the figures of three men, one of them raised something to his shoulder and *whoosh!* A streak of light headed for the cruiser. She closed her eyes but felt and heard the blast as the rocket hit the SUV and exploded.

Bonnie opened her eyes again as the smoke was starting to clear. She drew a bead on the man with the rocket launcher still on his shoulder. Bonnie squeezed the trigger, and her shot caught him in the upper arm on that side, just where she'd aimed.

He dropped the launcher, grabbing his wounded arm.

She hoped that would be enough to make them all spin and vamoose, but no such luck.

The deputy ran back to his burning and smoldering vehicle. He had his sidearm drawn and was looking both ways.

Bonnie rushed toward him and knocked him to the ground just as the other two men opened fire with handguns. She sprawled across the deputy, who struggled to get out from under her. She was by no means tall and was roundish with what she called a low center of gravity. Plus, she knew enough about wrestling to keep the deputy pressed down for a few ticks despite his determined squirming and some pretty salty shouting.

"Stay down!" She took her own advice, since it was harder to shoot down toward someone, and it was easier for her to swing the scope toward the flashes coming from the end of what sounded like an automatic. Bonnie squeezed, and the gun flew out of the man's hand.

The deputy managed to squirm free, but Bonnie didn't have to repeat her instruction. He sprawled next to her, raised his gun, and began to fire steadily in the direction of their opposition without pausing to take aim.

Gravel and dirt pressed into Bonnie's flesh, and she wished for a second she'd had the sense to go flat where there was grass. But it was not the time to think of creature comforts. The crackle of the flames that engulfed the cruiser filled the air as well as shots and shouting. The smell of the fire made her hope the sheriff's department vehicle wouldn't explode any more than it already had. She couldn't move any farther away from it without making a target of herself.

Then shots came from behind Bonnie. Al and Fergie were shooting as they ran. She recognized the sounds of Fergie's Glock and Al's SIG Sauer. They had a welcome ring to her ear. Then she heard a shotgun fire. Another shell was pumped into place, and it fired again. Maury was in a shooting stance, holding the Winchester.

"Get down, you fool!" Bonnie yelled at him. "You're small, but they might get lucky."

But the absolute fusillade had its effect, and the three men flat-out ran back up the lane as fast as they could go. Almost at once, they were out of the light of the burning cruiser and had disappeared.

The deputy beside her scrambled to his feet and ran up the lane toward the road. Al and Fergie went after him, while Maury came over to hold out a hand and help Bonnie up.

A truck peeled out, leaving some rubber and throwing gravel. She doubted the deputy's run was going to matter much.

"Is Little Al in his crib?" Bonnie asked Maury.

"And is asleep, unless all this hubbub roused him. I'll go back and have a look. Tanner wanted to come, too, always eager for a good time. You're all right?" He looked her over, as if expecting to find holes.

"Just dandy," she said, "and I'll prove it when we finally get to settle down. You can count on something extra special."

"Oh boy," he said. "Extra special." He headed back toward the house at a slow jog.

Bonnie pulled out her flashlight out and was looking at the ground when the deputy came back with Al and Fergie. He still held his pistol low in one hand. The name plate on his chest read Owens, and he looked to be one of the older deputies, so Al probably knew him.

"Did you see what they did to my cruiser?" He was staring at the smoldering, still-burning hulk, perhaps wondering how he would look if he'd stayed inside it and also pondering the report he was going to have to write.

"Yep, and here's what they did it with," Bonnie said.

The deputy, Fergie, and Al came closer to see where she was pointing her light. Her bright beam showed two boxes marked Mk 153. One of the rocket launchers was still in its box. The other was on the ground, where it had been dropped.

"My guess is they planned to take care of you then use the other one on the house with all of us in it." Bonnie's heart was still beating fast, partially from the thrill of thwarting their plan. "You'd best come to the house and use our phone there."

The deputy nodded, his expression still firm and thoughtful, perhaps at how close he'd come to being in that cruiser when it exploded.

"Fergie and I are going to make a swing around each side and come in the back way," Al said. "Just to make sure nobody is getting their courage up again."

They took off in different directions and were lost in the dark almost at once.

Bonnie turned to the deputy. "It's a good thing you had that call to nature when you did."

"You didn't...?"

"Naw. I looked away, like any gentleman or lady would," Bonnie said. "I was a nurse for years, so I didn't need to bone up on my anatomy studies. But I got a brief look at those jaspers through my scope and gave one or two of them something to remember me by. I imagine your crime scene crew can get some prints off the launcher."

"We already have a pretty good idea of who we're dealing with here," he said.

"C'mon, Deputy Owens." She gave a wave as she turned around.

He turned and started to follow her as she headed back toward the house, staying on the lane that time.

"You don't happen to have any coffee at the house, do you?"

"Sure we do."

"I expect I'll still be busy out here when the roosters are crowing."

"I wouldn't count too much on the kind of roosters we have near us. They're as apt to crow at noon as four a.m. Damnedest bunch of yard birds I've ever heard."

THE CRIME SCENE CREW was still going over the area, and a flatbed tow truck waited, with all kinds of colored lights flashing, to tow away what was left of Deputy Owens's ruined cruiser when Victor Kahlon pulled up in his truck. He got out and looked around.

Al and Fergie stood back a ways, letting the crime scene people work.

Victor took a quick peek into the crew's van, where they had already loaded the two rocket launchers, one still in its box, to take back to their lab. One of them was collecting footprint samples, while another was measuring distances.

Victor went around the busy crew and walked up to Al and Fergie. He looked up at the sky. "What is it Bonnie always says?"

"That it's as dark as the inside of a cow." Fergie glanced up. "Some cloud cover has moved in, and if my antique knees know anything, it might just rain."

"You're not antique."

"You know better than that. Al and I are both in our sixties and shouldn't be getting tangled up all the time with the kind of folks we're dealing with here."

"Come on up to the house," Al said. "Owens has already gotten a statement from Bonnie and has written one of his own. Did you check with any of the hospitals? Bonnie winged at least a couple of them."

"Is she getting off in her aim?"

"She hit what she was aiming at, as she usually does." Al turned and led the way up the lane.

"Did any of them return fire?"

"Yeah, but not for long. Owens joined Bonnie in returning fire before Fergie, Maury, and I came in like the cavalry. They were probably startled. Off balance," Al said. "I think the picture in their heads was to blow up the deputy's cruiser then come blow up my house. Having someone pop out of the woods with a rifle and wound one of them wasn't in their plan. They hadn't counted on the deputy being out of the cruiser either. Then they had to get out pronto and take their wounded with them."

"They're not going to be any happier," Victor said.

"These are not happy people in the first place," Fergie replied.

Victor was the same height as Al and realized he was looking up into Fergie's hazel eyes, which could show amusement and concern at the same time. A breeze lifted her long red hair before it fell back onto her shoulders. She was thin, the opposite of Bonnie's round plumpness.

As Fergie opened the front door to usher him into the house, Victor could hear Bonnie scolding Maury.

"What were you thinking, standing upright like that with bullets flying every which way? Do you want our boy to grow up without a father?"

The lights were all on. Victor looked around. Everything was nice and solid, neat and well cared for. It wasn't the home of a rich person, but it had the cozy, lived-in look he preferred. It would have been a shame if those guys had blown it up or burned it down. But that danger wasn't all the way over yet.

Bonnie and Maury were sitting at the dining table, cleaning and loading guns. Boxes of ammo sat on the table, and the dog was curled up at their feet. The baby was in a papoose on Maury's chest, asleep with his head pressed against Maury, who was busy loading shells into the Model 12 Winchester. It was nothing like a Norman Rockwell painting.

"Looks like you're getting ready for World War Seven," Victor said.

When Al and Fergie approached the table, they put their pistols on it for loading.

The dog rose to go to Al, who bent to pet his head. "I know you would have liked to be out there too. But someone had to stay back and guard Little Al."

"Al, I know you and the others may think this is some kind of jolly fun," Victor said, "but I want to caution you on how serious these jaspers are."

"They were just shooting at us. Is it more serious than that?" Fergie asked.

"Those rocket launchers mean more than just an escalation of armament," Victor said. "They indicate these may be—probably are—the ones who stole weapons from the nearest National Guard armory, where a man was killed. We think he may have been their inside connection, but the fact remains there's a murder charge to consider as well. Armed and dangerous hardly seems enough to describe these men."

"You should include 'pissed off' too," Bonnie said. "I never saw a bunch like this for holding a grudge."

"We were only going to have someone watching your place for a few days, and that's almost over."

Victor turned to Al. "Have you given any thought to taking off and staying somewhere else for a while?"

"And let them come and burn the place down?"

"But you'd still be alive."

"If they were coming for you, would you tuck your tail and go off and hide?"

Victor hesitated then said, "Probably not."

Al nodded.

"Sheriff Clayton has two concerns. He'd like to catch these people...alive, so they can stand trial. And he'd like to avoid you folks becoming vigilantes."

"Do you recall when the county commissioners were down on the people along a two-lane forty-five-mile-per-hour road who were putting up speed limit signs where vehicles were going way too fast and hitting deer, pets, and endangering children? The church even changed its sign to read 'This is God's country, so don't drive like hell through here.' The commissioners called those who were upset 'local vigilantes' at the time. But the commissioners still didn't put up more speed limit signs. Vigilantism occurs when people perceive that those in a position of power aren't doing something that they could or should."

"Can I just get your word you'll try to do what the sheriff wants?"

"Sure," Al said, "if you can get those other guys to agree to that first."

MAURY AND BONNIE STOOD close together, her shoulder pressed against his side with his arm around her. They looked down into Little Al's crib. He was sleeping. Maury couldn't believe sometimes that he had played a part in making anything so wonderful and magnificent as their son.

He turned to look at Bonnie, taking her in as if just meeting her. Her smooth, round face positively glowed, and while he'd known a lot of women, he found her plump, short body perfect. His own older hands looked a little withered and worn next to her smooth, taut-skinned ones. Yet there they were.

"I'm worried," he said.

"About them hurting us or Little Al?"

"More about what you might do to them."

"You think I might get sent away for plugging filth and effluvia like them?"

"Weirder things have happened. Besides, you know the sheriff wants these guys alive, and they all look at you when they say that."

"Are *you* afraid of me?"

"You will note that I have stayed faithful and true since we married. None of that roving-eye stuff for me anymore."

"Plus, I'm twenty-four years younger. I can outrun you and certainly outgun you."

"I think about that sometimes. I'm in my sixties. Will I still be around when Little Al graduates high school?"

"I don't think you even need to worry about such things," she said, "until these guys after us are dealt with. Then you can worry away to your heart's delight."

"Like I can keep from worrying."

"Come on. Get your mind off it." She took his hand and tugged him toward the bed. "How about something extra special?"

"Hoo boy. Extra special." He let himself be led.

Chapter Six

Ketchum pulled a folding chair closer to the kitchen table and sat carefully, leaning his cane against the side of his seat where he could get at it. The damned thing was a bother, but he would probably fall on his ass without it.

He leaned forward to watch Cable patching up Kale. Biff and Kale were the two with wounds. Ketchum sipped on a can of Budweiser that was starting to get warm. When he reached into his pocket for a Marlboro cigarette, he remembered he was trying to quit, another damn thing that pissed him off.

"Where'd you pick up all this medic stuff?" Kale looked down at the bandages Cable was wrapping around his grazed right hand.

The worst part, Kale had told Ketchum, was that the wound had caused him to drop his piece and leave it behind. That had been one sweet HK416, he'd said, the kind Delta Force used, and he didn't know where he would get another like it. He was still going to be able to shoot with that hand once patched up, so Ketchum wondered why he'd dropped the damn gun. *Prioritize, young man.*

"Didn't you learn anything in basic training?" Cable glanced up at Kale.

"Are you kidding? All I was studying back then was how to get a bra open with one hand while not looking."

"Well, in our unit, we were supposed to have at least one person able to back up our medic for the joy that was Desert Storm, and that was me. Jolly fun, that romp across the sand."

Biff dug into his small bag for the only other shirt he'd brought along. Cable had cut off the shirt he'd been wearing. It had a couple of holes in it anyway. Cable had patched his shoulder, front and back, where a rifle shot had made a clean through-and-through without hitting a bone. Biff had an awkward time getting into the shirt, but he didn't ask for help, although moving the arm with the fresh wound had to make it hurt like dammit.

Buff sat on the end of one of the twin beds. He crushed the empty beer can in his hand and tossed it into the corner of the room, which was already starting to look like it had been lived in hard. The Eagle's Nest fishing camp cabins were far from luxurious, but that didn't matter to them, and they were cheap.

"What kind of world is it when people won't stay put and let you blow them up?"

The room went as quiet as a grave for a couple of seconds. Then they all broke out laughing at once, even Ketchum. Buff was the last to catch on to what he'd said and was soon laughing the hardest of them.

"Whoever was shooting at us had to be using a scope to be this accurate," Cable said. "Next time, move around more. It's harder than blazes to hit a moving target with a scope, especially at night."

"One thing I'll agree on is that whoever shot at us was an expert-level shooter, maybe ex-military, like us." Biff glanced at the white bandages around his shoulder as he buttoned up his shirt.

"We're sure a sorry-lookin' lot," Ketchum said. "More'n half of us is shot up and hardly fit for combat, but we go on... if y'all are game." His right arm was in a cast, and he was painfully getting around with the help of that damned cane, but he didn't want to look weak in front of the others.

Buff crushed another already-empty can into a tight little ball and tossed it into the corner. "I am if you guys are."

The others each nodded with hardly any hesitation at all.

"Yeah, I could just as well be visiting my ex so she could be making hubby's hobby happen." Kale grinned. "But we all know that ain't gonna happen anytime soon. So I say we mess up these people instead."

"I wouldn't mind knowing a bit more about who these people are, shooting the way they did." Cable put the roll of zinc oxide tape and the box of gauze pads back into the small pouch he used as a first aid kit and put that in his backpack, which held all the worldly goods he'd brought along for their little adventure.

"I can help you there," Biff said. He was staring down at the screen of his cell phone. "You'll recall that when I was employed at the DMV, I found the address where that bitch Bonnie Quinn lived. The house belonged to a guy named Allard Quinn."

"The husband or father?" Ketchum asked.

"I don't think so. This Allard is married to a woman formerly named Ferguson Jergens, who people apparently call Fergie. Get this. She was a detective on the Austin Police Department."

"Aw man," Cable said.

"That made me loop back to this Quinn dude himself," Biff said. "Turns out he was a detective for the sheriff's department."

"That explains some of the shooting," Cable said.

"Do we back away from these folks?" Kale looked at Ketchum.

"Hell no! We just have to hit them harder and quicker. Be fast and hard enough to make their eyes pop."

He looked around at them. Buff just shrugged, while the others nodded. Cable even had an eager gleam in his eyes.

Ketchum said, "We lost some hardware and have to make a shopping trip to Heck Marmon's house." He was the one who owned and ran the shooting range.

"But he's our friend," Buff said. "We've shot at his place for years."

"Do you have a better idea? You've seen the security at gun shops these days. Besides, he told us to stay the hell away when last I jawed with him. The sheriff's department had been to visit. He told them all about us. Windy chap and a rat fink. So he's kinda got a debt to pay."

Ketchum was taking a chance there. They'd just been through a shoot-out where Purple Hearts would have been awarded, if they were legit. He was hoping they wouldn't lose the fire in their bellies. Looking around at them, he thought, *Nope, they're still as full of piss and vinegar as I am.* "Well, there is one other thing we could try first."

"What's that?" Buff asked.

Ketchum reached for his cane and used it to help himself up from the chair. "If you girls are tired of sitting on your hands and licking your wounds, c'mon. We're going to the docks."

"The ones where we saw the fishing boats parked, next to the boat ramp?" Buff might have been the biggest of them, but his mission in life seemed to be proving he wasn't the brightest by any means.

"Yep." Ketchum hobbled toward the door. "Almost surely some dumb cluck has left his keys hid somewhere on one of them." He paused and looked at Cable. "The marina will be locked and has one of those chain-link security gates. Do you think you can pick it or get around it?"

"Don't need to." Cable held up the key to the cabin the guy in the dirty sleeveless undershirt had given him when he rented it. "The second key goes to the docks, the assumption being that anyone staying at a fishing camp plans to do some fishing."

CABLE HELD UP ONE HAND to keep the spray out of his eyes. As they got closer, Ketchum had to ease slowly off the throttle. The wake behind them died out in silver moonlit streaks. Ketchum had insisted on driving, even though he had to reach across with his left hand to change the speed of the Bayliner with its big silver Honda motor. Cable had found the spare key to it, with a key float that read Stallings Marina, inside an unlocked hatch hidden under spare life vests. *Dumbass boaters.*

The boat, with its white deck and royal-blue hull, was a lucky find, since the five of them would have had a hard time fitting into one of the two-seat bass boats. They were crowded as it was, with Buff's bulk beside Ketchum.

As the boat got even closer, Ketchum turned the key and let the boat's momentum carry it toward Al Quinn's fishing dock.

Cable stood slowly in the bow, ready to keep them from bumping with a loud thump. When the bow was a foot from the edge, he leaped over onto the dock, holding the tender in one hand. With one foot, he kept the boat from hitting. Then he bent to fasten the tender to a cleat on the corner of the dock with a quick half-hitch knot. The aft end swung until the boat was parallel to the outside of the dock, and Biff could loop a line around the cleat near that end.

Cable was already easing up the hill toward the back of the house. By the time he got to the first level of cement steps, he could barely see the boat in the water when he glanced back. The night was dark enough to be good cover. He still had another level to go up to get to the house.

As he crested the edge of the lawn that led to the back door, he couldn't see any lights at all in the house. He eased to one side of the house and went up the hill until he was at the level of the front door. Still no lights inside, and he could see no vehicles parked in front. *Did they head for the hills after all?*

All the way back to the boat dock he stayed silent, keeping his feet on grass where he could. He was supposed to give an all clear if the place was right for an attack.

When Cable was close enough to the boat dock for Ketchum to see him, he shook his head and held up a zero sign with one hand, indicating no one was at home.

Ketchum gestured back the act of lighting a match and pointed back toward the house. There was no need for all of them to go if it was going to be that simple.

Cable went silently back up to the house in the nearly black night. He gathered the driest leaves and twigs he could find and made a small pile of them beside the back door, where the flame would reach up to the wood. Though he would've liked a bit of paper to start the fire, he had seen none lying around. *Damn neat freaks.* So he took a folded wad of bills from his pocket and peeled off a one-dollar bill to use as a paper starter.

From his other pocket, he pulled out a book of matches and bent low over the pile of leaves and tinder to shelter it from the wind.

Just as he started to strike a match, a bullet hit the concrete of the porch right in front of him and screamed as it ricocheted away.

His combat reflexes kicked in, and he rolled over backward and scrambled to get flat then scurry away as fast as he could. He went right over some burrs and probably a cactus or two before he got to the stairs, keeping his head down as he ran down both sets as fast as he could go.

As he got to the dock, he waved for the others to untie the boat. When they were slow to spring to the task, he leaped onto the bow, pulled out his belt knife, which he kept sharp enough to shave with, and slashed the tender. Then he scrambled to the aft end and cut that tie. "Just go!" he yelled. "And go like hell!"

Ketchum turned on the engine, ignoring the noise it would make, and shot away from the dock, heading across the lake in a roar and a near rooster tail of a wake.

BONNIE CAME OUT OF the woods carrying the 30-06 rifle. She was comforted knowing Maury was safe, having gone off with the baby and Tanner in Fergie's car.

Fergie and Al came from the other side. Al was slipping his SIG Sauer inside his belt at the small of his back. Fergie still held her Glock down at her side.

"I'm glad you didn't wait until he lit that match and had the house burning," Al said.

Bonnie picked the dollar bill out of the starter pile. "I just knew he'd be one cheap tipper."

"But ho, ho. What's that?" Al pointed at the paper book of matches lying on the porch.

Bonnie picked it up. "Eagle's Nest Fish Camp," she read.

Fergie chuckled. "That's what ol' Sherlock would have called a clue. A damned simple-minded thing of them to do."

"Well, these guys are hardly *rocker* scientists," Bonnie said.

"But give them this—they can damn well hold on to a mad as well as anyone I've ever met." Al took out his phone and started punching in Victor Kahlon's number.

ONCE AGAIN, CABLE WAS catching a lot of spray as they went, even more than before. But he didn't mind, as long as they were moving and moving fast.

Ketchum didn't slow the boat until they were nearly back to the fishing camp. As soon as the noise of the motor slowed to a low rumble, he glanced back toward Cable. "We heard shots. Thought they might've got you up there."

"If that shooter wanted me dead, I'd be dead." Cable was still shaking, adrenaline rippling through him like a herd of scampering mice. "They could have killed me, but they didn't. What the hell's up with that?" He felt no fear, just knew his body was going through the usual adjustment after a battle, the way he'd felt overseas after taking horrible risks yet coming out alive.

Cable hopped out and held the boat while the others climbed onto the dock, Ketchum taking the longest time. He wasn't fooling anyone. He was about as spry as a door mat.

As soon as they were all on the dock, Cable let the boat drift. He'd already cut away the ties.

Up in their cabin, they moved quickly, even Ketchum, who was suppressing winces with each step.

Kale picked up a damp towel and started wiping down surfaces.

"What're you doing that for?" Ketchum snapped. "They already know who we are by now."

"Best not make it too easy for them." But Kale tossed the towel aside as they all headed for the door.

Like the others, he was fine with fueling his own purpose by feeding off Ketchum's sustained anger. The fire in that belly rarely flickered low. They were all in the same boat, and none of them were complaining. Cable had found himself on the wrong side of the law a time or two, as they all had.

"*Assault?*" he'd shouted at the judge when he was facing charges for dragging a man outside a two-step kicker bar and cutting off his man bun with a knife. "I'm practically a barber, and don't tell me you like those damn things." So that ended up being time served for, as he put it, "Doing hardly nothing."

Cable looked around at them. At first glance, Biff seemed like any other son of the South he might meet on the street, except for his eyes. Those were narrow and beady, like a snake's. They always seemed to be busy, considering and plotting, and were far from full of what anyone could call warmth or human kindness.

He'd heard Biff tell Ketchum, "All my life, I been wanting things just out of reach or not right for me. When I was married—good-looking wife—I wanted someone else's wife. Want, want, want. I was like a dog chasing cars yet couldn't drive one if he caught one. I wasn't one of them pretty boys, but I wanted the same things they wanted. Wasn't gonna happen. Now I don't know what's gonna happen to us or me. But this feels right, like the fight we gotta fight. Someone's gotta get hurt. Someone's gotta pay."

Buff, on the other hand, often had a blank stare that hinted that wind might be whistling into one ear and out the other. That was, unless he had the opportunity to pull the legs off something or someone. Then he looked a little more animated and eager. He had the lamest and potentially funny—though not to him—rap sheet of them. Some Shirley Temple of a little girl knocking at his door had somehow convinced him to donate to a charity. Then someone—Cable seemed to recall it was Kale—called Buff a sucker by telling him what the CEOs of charities make and had even shown him a website detailing what vast amounts were going into the pockets of fat cats from the nickels and dimes donated by people who scrimped and saved so they could feel like they were making a contribution to doing some good.

Leaders of so-called non-profit organizations had salaries in the multimillions. In the name of fighting cancer, heart disease, and even domestic violence, they were raking in hefty percentages of donations given in good faith, financing some pretty rich lifestyles. Kale had found an article or two that showed the mansion homes and fancy yachts of some of the well-off CEOs of charities. He poured the details on thick for Buff until they made him feel even more of an idiot than he already believed himself to be and told him it made him and so many others just gullible fools.

That lit a fuse under Buff that led to his throwing a cinder block to crash through the front window of a Goodwill store, then stealing the pot of money from a shopping mall Santa. But the thing he eventually got busted for was smashing apart a United Fund billboard with a sledgehammer he stole from a nearby construction site. He'd been caught in the act though not in time to save the sign.

The truth was ol' Buff just wanted someone or something to be mad at, like all of them. They loved hate. They fed off it. Hate was the fire in the furnace of their bellies, whether about politics, any football team other than the Dallas Cowboys or even the Houston Texans, or anyone who crossed their paths and needed their attitude hammered to the ground.

Cable, like his pals, fed off the others' anger.

Damn, it all makes me feel pumped up, full of purpose, and ready to bite the head off a snake.

As a rule, Cable was only out to teach people a harsh lesson. Of course, he had killed before, a few times, but had done so discreetly and, he thought, tastefully.

Is it wrong, he had once asked himself, *to feel a wave of happiness when someone who gave you a hard time passes away? Especially if you're the one who helped them along with that?*

Ketchum, well, he was more than just a little road rage incident being escalated when those he was mad at refused to make it easy for him to get satisfaction. He was a model for being mad, for hating, and for just being a plain festering boil on the side of what otherwise would be a peaceful society. Cable had to admire that.

"Time to scramble!" Ketchum's voice was like the crack of a whip. "This night's far from over."

Chapter Seven

Victor Kahlon and two other units from the sheriff's department swooped in on the Eagle's Nest Fish Camp as soon as they could get there. They pulled in with lights flashing and sirens blaring.

He'd called ahead to get the cabin number and caution the camp's manager not to go near it until he and the other deputies got there.

Of course, the damned fool had ignored his instructions and gone inside with what looked like a snow shovel and a big black heavy-duty plastic bag. He was loading scoops of beer cans and the litter that covered the floor into the bag.

"Put that shovel down, and back out of there!" Victor said. The smell of the place—stale sweat, beer, and man stink—came out and hit him like a wave. Beer cans, empty bean cans, and fast-food wrappers covered the floor and countertops.

The manager looked up at him. "What?"

"You're contaminating evidence."

"Of what?"

"Just step outside for a moment or two."

The man leaned the shovel against the wall and let go of the edge of the open bag to reach up and pull at the remaining hair on his nearly bald head. "Damn tomfools. Gonna take me a week to clean the stink outta this cabin. Fishermen ain't no neat freaks as a rule, but these guys? Whew. I gotta rent this place again, don't ya know."

Victor waved the reluctant man out. He didn't really think they would find much except a few confirming fingerprints. But he would have liked to go through the place when it was fresh, maybe find some idea of where the birds might go next. All he knew for the moment was that Ketchum and his cohorts were long gone.

He looked around at the shambles they'd left behind. *Man, how can they live like this?* Someone tall had written BITCH in block letters high on one wall where the paneling was cracking. A very sharp knife had stabbed through and left a hole in an empty can of gun oil. It was surely a hate-fueled little cell that must have been a joy to sleep in and hang out in.

The other deputies started tossing the place for anything that might give them a lead to where the gang might go next. He joined in but soon shook his head. He agreed with the camp's manager. *What a sty!* But they could find nothing.

As they went back outside, the manager said, "Coulda told ya. I've had guys clean fish indoors and still leave the place nicer than these a-holes. Hey, and someone cut loose one of the docked boats and set it adrift. We had to go out after it. Found it a quarter mile upwind of here. Do you think it was these guys?"

"Could well be. Do you want to file a report?"

"Naw. Too much damn paperwork. We got the boat back, no thanks to them scum."

Victor had climbed into his truck with the sinking feeling that the clock was ticking faster and he was going to have to start over from scratch. That and the department's surveillance of Al's house was coming to the end of its short-lived stretch, having produced little, unless they counted getting one of their cruisers blown up. The matchbook clue had been the first clear crack at finding the men, but it had fizzled. They'd been as quick and wary as hunted foxes.

Perhaps the sheriff's department could claim a tiny victory in recovering the weapons robbed from that armory, but that wasn't even in their county, so that, too, was a shallow victory at best. Plus, Clayton was keeping the pressure on to find the men and make an example of them.

BONNIE CAME IN THE front door of their house two evenings later, carrying the 30-06. Al looked up from where he was on his knees beside Tanner, checking to ensure the wrappings showed no leakage. Tanner was licking the back of Al's hand.

"Well, they're gone," she said. "I guess we're on our own now."

"The sheriff department support?"

She nodded.

"Just as well," Al said. "I felt kind of guilty about their spending taxpayers' money on the likes of us. Besides, as we found out, a single deputy posted in the lane isn't going to stop these men. They seem a determined and nasty lot."

"I can't disagree with you," Fergie said from the kitchen, where she was putting away dishes. "But I do kind of wonder where they are now and what they're up to."

Bonnie looked around at the house she called home. It was a warm and cozy place where she had been pleased to raise her young son in safety. *Until now.* She had a quick flash of a thought, one she'd had before. *Yeah, this place is worth fighting for.*

All of Bonnie's family was long gone, so Al, Fergie, Maury, and Little Al were her family now. She looked them over. Al was petting his dog but looking as hard as flint. Fergie was just as tough but more prone and able to show warmth and human kindness.

Fergie's face was slender and fair. She had retained enough of the glow and innocence of her long-ago youth to be quite attractive when relaxed and content.

Bonnie had seen the faces of some women who worked the streets go from innocent to worldly-wise with a sarcastic edge within a year of entering that occupation full time.

Her own round face could still project some youthful joy of life.

Sure, she and Fergie had seen and experienced some things that would make a deacon's hair stand on end like a porcupine's. But they had avoided becoming hard and sinister. She attributed some of that to them both having the love of good men, Al and Maury.

She'd only caught a glimpse or two of that Ketchum fellow but thought he'd looked as mean as a snake with a butt full of cactus needles.

"One of us is going to have to be on watch constantly now," Al said. "We'll need to do shifts."

Maury came around the corner, having come up from downstairs. He held a finger to his lips. The baby was asleep at last. He was Al's older brother by a year, and Bonnie was a good twenty-some years younger than him. Maury had been a horndog and a woman chaser, including that nasty business with Al's wife, but she felt she had tamed him somewhat. He had become a faithful father and part of a loving nuclear family. *Big strides for someone with his past.*

He must have overheard them. He went over to the front door, where the shotgun leaned against the wall. "I'll take first watch," he said, "but make it happen with the watch shifts where I get some time later with Bonnie. I'm a man with needs, I tell you."

Bonnie sniffed the air and glanced at the clock. "That pie in the oven's just about ready. Why don't you wait and have a slice of that with a cup of coffee before you head out there."

"Is that all I have time for?" He put the gun back down beside the door.

"It'll have to do for now. But later, maybe we can wrangle some catch-up time."

"Oh goodie. Catch-up... and perhaps some mustard."

Bonnie rolled her eyes at Al and Fergie. "Sometimes he can be like a seven-year-old with a sex drive. I don't know why I find that strangely attractive and endearing, but I do."

"I'll go along with strange," Fergie said.

HECK MARMON LIVED IN a hundred-year-old house at the back of a long lane that passed right by his shooting range. He'd inherited one hundred forty-seven acres that had been cattle range back when his grandpappy first settled on it.

Ketchum drove the dark-blue Silverado pickup they'd "borrowed" from a truck stop parking lot before they'd put the last of their own trucks in storage lockers, where they would probably have to stay as long as the heat was on. His own truck was still in that damned sheriff's department impound lot, a fact that only stoked the fire inside him. Dawn wasn't too far away, and he was tired to his bones, especially the throbbing ones of his healing right arm. He had hobbled about too much with the cane, too, and his leg felt like it had been touched by a burning ember. But he wanted to ride the mad that was driving him. It was like a good adrenaline or alcohol buzz, only better, grittier, and more real. He felt more alive than ever.

His headlights lit up a thick chain with a Keep Out sign stretched across the end of the lane as he pulled the truck off the road. They knew one end of the chain was only looped over the top of one post. Biff got out of the truck's passenger seat, walked to the right post, slipped the chain loop off, and let the chain drop to the ground. As soon as Biff was back in the truck and had closed his door, Ketchum headed up the lane.

To get to the house, he had to drive past the shooting range, where they'd spent many an hour and round of ammunition, then go back a long way, down a winding lane and through a thick copse of live oaks and cedar.

He could see the house ahead at last, peeking out from the trees that surrounded it. Heck Marmon sure hadn't wasted a lot of time and money painting the place. Ketchum turned off the headlights then the engine. He didn't have to tell the others to be quiet. They knew.

As he stepped out of the truck and let the cane take some of his weight, he looked up at a windy, weird sky with torn shreds of clouds skittering across it, giving only brief glimpses of the moon. So far out from all the usual light pollution, he would have been able to see the stars easily and make out the Little Dipper, which was about the only constellation he knew by name. He could smell the cattle first then heard an occasional lowing. Heck kept half a dozen longhorn steers in the fenced-off pastures at the back of the property. He had the devil's own time keeping a few of the overenthusiastic patrons from slipping back there and plugging one of them.

Cable led the way to the house and, without being told, went around to the back to block the exit from that direction. He carried a Colt .45 automatic he'd had for as long as any of them remembered.

Biff and Kale had pistols. Buff had none. That was why they were at the house, for a little shopping trip.

When they got to the front door, Ketchum stood off to one side and waved his cane hand at Buff.

Buff stood back and tossed a rock the size of a grapefruit at the front door. A shotgun blast from inside blew a hole through Heck's door. The shot would have finished anyone fool enough to try to just open the door.

"I knew it'd be rigged," Ketchum said. "Let's go."

Kale reached inside the hole and unlocked the door.

They rushed in, Ketchum glancing left and right, taking in the sparsely furnished empty front room. He knew Cable wouldn't be foolish enough to try coming in the back way just yet.

Heck came staggering out of his bedroom while pulling on blue jeans, a modesty that was going to cost him.

Ketchum let his cane fall to one side, drew a Smith & Wesson .38 out of the front of his belt, and shot Heck in the belly.

Heck fell onto his back, staring up at them in disbelief. "You guys? What the...?"

Without needing to move closer, Ketchum shot him in the face.

Buff winced, probably from a brief thought that Heck had been their friend. But he clearly got over that in a second and went with the others to a spare bedroom where Heck kept some of his guns as well as ammo he sold if anyone needed some at the range.

Ketchum shoved the pistol back under his belt and bent to get his cane. He smiled when he stood upright and saw a grenade launcher, an M320 like he'd used himself a time or two. It leaned beside a row of three AR-15s, an M16, and an AK-47 in a wooden gun rack. There would be no opening the huge gun safe, since Heck was no longer alive, but boxes of all manner of ammunition filled the shelves beside it.

"Dibs on the M16. Be sure to get that case of grenades too," he told Buff.

Cable came into the room, having gone around the house to come in the front way. None of them mentioned Heck as they picked out weapons and what matching ammo they could for the jolly times ahead. Kale had even found a Heckler & Koch 416 just like the one he'd had to leave behind earlier. He grinned, looking as happy as a kid at Christmas as he scooped up all the ammo he could get for it.

Ketchum hobbled with his cane around Heck's body and looked into the bedroom. He shook his head. The room was nearly empty except for an army cot covered by a military blanket against one wall. "We did the man a favor. Imagine living like this."

A small wooden stand with a lamp that stood within reach of the pillow end of the cot also held a small clock, a Korth Combat .357 revolver, and Heck's wallet.

He should have gone for the gun instead of his pants, Ketchum thought. When he picked up the wallet, he found only seven hundred dollars inside. He took that, hoping the break-in might pass as a robbery. The Korth, an upscale German version of the Colt Python, was one of the most expensive revolvers available. He slid it under his belt next to the S&W. A lot of the ammo was probably in the gun safe, as was much of Heck's money. He wished he could get at that. Business had been good for Heck since the state had passed a law allowing Texans to carry handguns without a license or training. Lots of people had been coming out to the shooting range to learn how to shoot.

Ketchum smiled, remembering how in the sixties and seventies, it had been common for Texas trucks to have gun racks in the back window, which often carried rifles or shotguns. While the practice had never been outlawed, enough guns had been stolen that loaded guns in a back window was no longer a smart idea.

A guy at the shooting range had once told him about how he'd been flipped off by a guy in a pickup. He'd shot the guy's back window out. When the truck went veering off the road and smashed into a big-ass tree, he went to the truck and found the driver unconscious, his face turned into bleeding hamburger by broken glass. So the shooting-range guy stole a pretty nice shotgun and rifle out of the back window and headed off down the highway. *Happy times!* He'd showed Ketchum the rifle, a Winchester Model 92 lever-action 30-30—John Wayne's favorite, a pretty nice gun. He hadn't even asked if Ketchum might be a cop or something, probably because Ketchum's look was just about the opposite of a cop's, except for the hard edge.

Ketchum knew he could count on the owner of just about every vehicle with an NRA sticker on the back window to have a weapon or two stowed somewhere in their home, if they had to go the burglary route.

Biff had moved their stolen truck closer, and they loaded what they could into it. Cable had found a tarp somewhere so they could conceal anything they needed to put in the truck bed. Buff had one of the AR-15s slung over his shoulder. Ketchum handed him his S&W, since he had just acquired the Korth for himself. Besides, the S&W was officially a murder weapon, one he'd just as soon not have on himself.

He climbed back into the driver's seat as Cable splashed gas from a can across the front of the house. The others climbed in, and Ketchum backed up the truck. Cable threw on a match and came running as flames licked up the front of Heck's place like hungry, angry tongues.

The sky glowed in the rearview mirror as Ketchum pulled out onto the road. He was sure going to sleep well once they'd unloaded the truck and switched out vehicles. He could still feel the steady fire of anger churning in his stomach but knew that even with his insides going like a furnace, he was tired enough to sleep well and long.

Chapter Eight

Victor had to wait for a black Ram 3500 truck pulling a flatbed trailer with a backhoe on it to come out the end of Al's lane before he could pull his truck into the drive. A pea-soup-thick fog had covered the back roads near the lake at not quite six a.m.

He had only gone about half the distance to the house when Al stepped out from behind a tree into the lane. He stood with a shotgun held low in his left hand, probably his Winchester Model 12. Victor figured Al had his SIG Sauer tucked in at the small of his back as well.

Al came around to stand beside Victor's open window. "Howdy." Al nodded.

"Back at you." Victor noticed two other men slowly coming out of the misty woods from where Al had emerged. "Well, as I live and breathe. Meat Jenkins and Huff." He had nearly called him "Dirty Fingernails Huff"—what everyone else called him, often to his face. *What a pair.* Huff wore a long-sleeve gray sweatshirt that looked like both sleeves had been used as a handkerchief, and he had a raccoon perched on one shoulder and what looked like a weasel hugging close to him on the ground near one Levi pant leg. Huff was carrying a nearly empty spool of black cord.

Victor had to admit that the two of them floating out of the mist like that had an eerie feel. He'd been worried about Al and his family being in the path of what he considered a dangerous and enraged handful of men. But he was starting to get the notion that perhaps Al's little group might just be able to take care of themselves. And he was damned if he could muster up anything like sympathy for the ones threatening Al.

He shook his head at the roundish Jenkins, who had a thick black beard and shiny white teeth, one of which was covered with just the hint of something like a bit of blueberry. "What are you doing out here, Meat? Don't you still work for the department?"

Where Meat was round and neat, Huff was skinny as well as somewhat scruffy by comparison. *Unlikely duo.* Both were the sort who were called nerds or geeks by high school classmates, and Al was just the sort to befriend such men. Meat was the IT specialist for the sheriff's department and had worked there back when Al was a detective, one of the best at what he did.

"Well, it was my day off, and Al is an old friend."

"Plus there was some sort of treat involved?" Victor asked.

"A blueberry pie and a turtle cheesecake."

"Part of which is already gone, I'll bet." Victor grinned. He knew Meat's weakness for sweets.

"The pie is pretty much history."

"And you, Huff, what brings you out to join this motley crew?"

"He's helping out with a varmint problem," Al said. "In addition to the techie stuff he and Meat enjoy, ol' Huff is wicked good at dealing with varmints, although he is prone to befriend many of them."

"Not these." Huff snorted.

Victor had a pretty clear notion of what he meant.

"What brings you out this way?" Al asked. "From what I gather through the media, someone did a number on Heck Marmon. His neighbors said it was like a fireworks display, and the volunteer fire department couldn't get near the house for a few hours. You have a good ID on the body?"

"Yeah, it's Heck all right, burnt down to a black cinder with two new bullet holes."

"Think it was the guys who are messing with my family?"

"You know how that is, Al. I don't think anything officially yet. Neither would you if you were in my shoes, which you have been. Not a fingerprint to be found, and even any footprints had been swept away by someone damned good at sweeping. All we have for sure is that who-ever did in Heck and torched the place came in a pickup truck. But in my head, all the pieces fit. The guy rats them out, and on top of that probably had all kinds of hardware, like that armory hit."

Al shook his head. "So you're suspecting what I'm thinking, that these guys have been active. Have struck again. I guess it doesn't pay to be friends with these guys."

"Or enemies," Victor said.

"There's that. Any luck finding them?"

"Not yet."

"I feared as much."

Victor rubbed his nose. "We have to have something to act on, like a complaint, a situation, or a crime. Well, we have that now, we think, or at least suspect so, and we're looking and looking hard. But there's not much we can do, unless we can find them, and we've had no luck with that so far."

"So it's kind of sit and wait until they strike?" Al asked.

"Pretty much. If I were you, I'd pack up what you value most, head out of these hills, and go to West Texas or up to the panhandle. Hunker down with the flatlanders for a spell."

"And let them burn down my house and who knows what else?"

"You'd be trading that for your lives. These guys, if it's them, are showing no compunction about killing outright now."

"I guess the department's token watch on my place didn't pan out and probably won't be used again."

"Clayton's already got a chapped butt about losing a cruiser. You know how much one of those Interceptor SUVs runs, especially with a full set of gear inside. So, not cheap."

CABLE WAS ALREADY WIPING down every surface of the truck's interior as they eased up to the side street beside a convenience store in South Austin. The place was a bodega really, given the area, which was three-quarters Hispanic, from what he'd read. As soon as Kale turned off the truck's engine, Cable tilted his head, putting it halfway out the open window, and listened.

"Bingo," he said.

A truck's engine was running in the store's parking lot. Kale moved his hands away and let Cable wipe the keys and steering wheel. "It's not like we're not leaving the unfortunate dude a vehicle," he said, "if he just bothers to look around."

They walked nonchalantly to the white Ford F-150 truck, which had its AC going. The goof hadn't even bothered to lock the doors. They had waited until midafternoon in the heat of the day when people were prone to leave engines running, one of the single biggest reasons for vehicle theft. A quick search of the internet told them that the areas with the greatest number of car thefts were in South Austin. But that didn't mean the cops were more vigilant in those areas about catching the thieves.

Cable, in the passenger seat, kept an eye on the front of the convenience store as Kale pulled out into traffic. No one came running out of the store, waving their arms or anything. He chuckled. It was so like the media in their lust to share a story that they practically told people where and how to go about the perfect crime of vehicle theft. Hell, he'd even seen detailed info on how to steal a Kia or Hyundai by using a USB cable to turn the ignition tumbler, start the car, and turn off the steering lock. *Boom!* The thing was they didn't want either of those. They wanted big American trucks. He and Ketchum had both done a little of their military time in Korea, and they'd just as soon take a bath in kimchi as drive one of those small foreign vehicles.

"Don't forget. We've gotta swing by that army surplus place and pick up five camo outfits," Kale said.

Cable glanced behind them. Still no one back there. "Camo? Isn't this gonna be a night thing? Black would probably work as well or better."

"Maybe so, but I think Ketchum kinda likes the idea of camo. You know, to build up the esprit de corps or something."

"Camo. Black. I doubt it all matters a hill of beans. We're gonna be in and out. Boom. Boom."

"Yeah. Boom-boom indeed."

Almost two hours later, they pulled into a gravel drive barely a couple of miles away from Al Quinn's drive.

"Wouldn't those assholes about crap a biscuit if they knew we were camped out practically in their backyard." Kale chuckled.

"Might be easier this way to sneak in without them getting any kind of drop on us." Cable slowed the newly acquired truck and eased up to the run-down single-wide trailer. He'd been damn lucky to find the place, which he suspected was abandoned. Someone had knocked down a For Sale sign that had been beside the end of the lane by the road. He'd moved that behind a tree and sprinkled leaves on it. From the dirt and dust in the interior, he figured no one had been out that way in a spell, nor would they be coming soon.

It had been a good run to town. He was humming a country song, something about the devils in your backyard. He had a lot of talents, in addition to scouting, hunting, and shooting. Cable felt he could have been a country star, singing at the Grand Ol' Opry and with Dolly Parton's head resting on his shoulder. Well, maybe it wouldn't be her head.

The door to the trailer swung open. Ketchum nodded at the truck they'd gotten. He started down the makeshift wooden steps, his cane hooked over the elbow of the arm with the cast and his good hand clinging to the rail someone had made out of PVC pipe.

"Get inside, and get what rest you can," Ketchum said. "We've got a big night ahead of us."

"Do you think someday folks will be singing songs about us?" Kale asked. "You know, ballads about bravery and such."

Ketchum tilted his head. "I had this writer sort of dude ask me once if I had a choice, would I want to be a hero, a victim, or a villain. I pondered over that some. My story would be that at first, I'd be a victim, which I am here, so I would have to become a villain to eventually be a hero."

"You think you're hero material?" Kale asked.

"I sure enough do."

AL AND FERGIE SAT ON the couch, their thighs touching. They looked in the direction of the television but hadn't turned it on. Tanner, with his prominent white bandage Al had recently changed, had curled up on the floor with his head on Al's feet and the rest of him stretched across Fergie's feet.

"Do you think it would be a terrible thing if we lit a few candles?" she asked.

"I think we can manage that. We have enough to get us through the next power outage or two and an evening like this. Do you want me to light a fire in the fireplace?"

"Not right now. But the candles would be nice."

He stood up and managed to extricate his feet from under Tanner, who looked up at him but stayed put.

Al came back with two white tapered candles in silver frog candle holders. He put them on the coffee table, lit them, and settled back on the couch, putting his arm around Fergie. She leaned closer. Tanner lifted his head and put it back on Al's feet.

"Do you ever think much about those twenty years that went by when you and Maury didn't speak to each other?"

"Now it seems more of a waste of time we could have spent together than it did at the time."

"But you were eventually forgiving. That's the key difference between you and these men who are bugging us."

"I think there are a few more differences than just that."

"How often did you see him?"

"Very little. By mutual consent, we stayed away from each other. Him because he thought I might just kill him."

"Would you have?"

"I was pretty angry. But I don't have it in me. That's another key difference between me and the men we're facing. Sure, I have killed, while in the service overseas and in self-defense when working on the sheriff's department. But my own brother? No. I heard about him and his exploits. He was sure a real horndog for that stretch. If he was carving notches on his bed posts, I doubt he had any posts after a while. Someone slashed his tires once, probably a husband or maybe a jilted woman. The thing that almost killed him was someone slipped three Viagra pills into his beverage, and him with a bad heart. The doctor thought that perhaps Maury might have been just 'ambitious.' You know how that led to Bonnie being his nurse. She sure has changed him for the good. That alone eventually let Maury and me reunite."

"What did *you* do for all that time?" Fergie asked.

"Oh, you know. I worked a lot. I went to the gym. I went fishing. I bought this place and fixed it up some. I had a few beers, but I'd hardly call myself much of a drinker. And you?"

"I'm really sad to admit that during the same block of time, my life was pretty much like yours. It just plodded along."

"But it's better now?"

"Yeah, it's much better... if we make it out the other end of what we're going through now."

Chapter Nine

When Ketchum woke from a deeper sleep than he'd expected to have, getting all the way awake was like pulling aside hazy red curtains before realizing he was in the trailer's full-sized bed. He took a slow inventory of his throbbing leg and reached to feel the arm in a cast. His thoughts solidified and centered on one thing, his driving purpose. *I'm going to take out that bitch and everyone around her... tonight.*

The inside of the trailer was dark except for a light somewhere at the far end. He knew it was night even before he glanced at his watch to see it was three a.m.

The others all lay on the floor, already in their camo outfits, except Cable, who was stretched out on the couch that ran along one side of the living room by the small breakfast nook.

He could hear Buff's steady deep snoring. But above that was a steady low grumble of thunder, more like it had an upset stomach than that it was angry. That was okay. He was angry enough for both himself and the damned sky.

As if in answer, the spatter of the first few drops hit the metal top of the trailer. Then the sky let loose with all it had, and the downpour of one real frog-walloper of a storm started to hammer the roof like a whole room of madcap drummers or frenzied marchers.

Dammit. Then he paused as he slowly forced himself to sit upright. *This could be good. We could use this.* The storm had come like a gift of an even better cover than just the dark of night.

The second he went out into the living area, Cable's eyes snapped open, and he sat up on the couch, one hand going down to feel the sheath of his belt knife. Without a word, he rose and started to wake the others. "It's showtime."

They all awakened the way soldiers did when out on a mission. They'd grabbed what winks they could and felt the urgency of a mission. Barely taking time to rub the sleep out of their eyes, they started checking their weapons and making sure they had all the ammo they would need.

Kale made sure the Heckler & Koch he held like a small child was ready to chatter. Cable had been careful to tape Kale's wounded right hand so that he could still grasp a rifle and pull the trigger. The H&K was fairly hair triggered, so all it needed was a gentle squeeze.

Cable had an AR-15 and the M16 he would carry for Ketchum, who would need to use a cane to get there. Buff had picked out the grenade launcher and had half a dozen grenades hanging from his belt by their pins. He seemed to barely notice his bandaged shoulder and looked as fit and ready as any of them. The glint in his eyes said he was hoping to make a big bang soon.

Without a pep talk, reassurance, or a word of any kind, they formed up, and Ketchum led the way out the door into a rain so hard it nearly knocked him down as he struggled down the slick wooden steps, grasping the PVC railing. As his boots landed on the mud and puddles of the trailer's yard, he reminded himself that the deluge was their friend, their mask in the night.

They took off in a tight bunch, slipping and sloshing through mud, deep wet grass, and dead leaves and sticks too damp to snap. Ketchum had envisioned Cable being twenty yards ahead of them, bent low and scouting as they crossed through woods and over other lakeside properties, staying away from any lights or places where they could be seen from windows. Instead, they could stay close together and make a reasonably straight beeline to their destination.

Rain hammered down on them. Walking through it was like parting the steel lines of a silver curtain. *This is no damn time to have to be using a cane.* He nearly fell a couple of times but couldn't imagine the shame of having to be helped back up. That tightened his resolve and steadied his footsteps, making him more careful.

At the edge of the target property, they slowed, forming an even tighter bunch. Ketchum held up a hand. They waited while Cable slipped ahead, disappearing almost at once in the slanting lines of rain. There was also a wind, and their camo outfits weren't made for warmth. Ketchum was already soaked to the skin and maneuvered to stand alee of Buff, using his bulk as a weather shield.

Cable suddenly appeared among them once more. They all moved their heads closer while he spoke in a low voice. "There's a pit or two and trip wires." He had been combat savvy enough to look for them. "Watch for punji stakes too. I didn't spot any, but this guy's seen combat in jungles like us."

They started again, moving slowly and cautiously, with Cable leading and all of them staying close.

Ketchum couldn't imagine anyone from the house being out on a night watch in the quagmire he and his group were wading through, but he kept a sharp watch all the same.

Cable stopped ahead of him and pointed downward. Ketchum found some firm ground and leaned on his cane. He couldn't see what he was pointing at, but Cable moved his hands apart like he was pulling at a wire. Ketchum nodded, not that it did a hell of a lot of good in all the noise and pouring rain.

Just a few steps farther, and Cable pointed out a pit right beside them. Ketchum didn't see it at first but then could make out a dark spot on the ground partially covered by a few frail limbs. *A beginner Boy Scout could make a better trap than that.*

The others were probably as restless and eager to get at the business they'd come to do as Ketchum was, but he made himself wait on Cable, who seemed able to see in the dark. Ketchum wanted to feel down in his own side pocket to run a hand over the flashlight there, but he needed his good hand on the cane. Being gimped up and half-crippled by those people only made the anger inside him burn brighter.

Kale must have had enough of being slow and cautious. He eased out on his own around the trip cord and pit Cable had indicated.

Just as Ketchum was preparing to risk yelling at him, Kale shot straight up into the dark sky as if he were rocket propelled.

It had happened so fast it looked like magic, but Ketchum knew it wasn't. He had set snare traps like that himself. Kale's ankle had probably gotten caught by a loop of black 1/8 inch Kevlar cord that yanked him into the air. That was the way he would have done it.

As suddenly as Kale had gone airborne, spotlights snapped on all around them, pointing down at where they stood and piercing through the thick sheets of rain with blinding lights. They turned the ground, trees, leaves, and mud a bright white, dimpled by the still falling rain.

Kale began to yell from where he bobbed in the air a good twenty feet above the ground and opened fire in all directions with his Heckler & Koch 416.

"Cut it out!" Ketchum yelled. He had dropped to the ground and crawled to sprawl behind the nearest big tree trunk, with some kind of stickers stabbing him through his pants leg. "You're gonna hit one of us."

But Kale didn't pause. He kept firing until his clip was empty. Then he jammed another clip into place.

"Stop, I said!"

Kale ignored him. He began firing away again in all directions, high and low, putting out sprays of shots that kicked up dead limbs and leaf litter.

Biff was the most exposed. He leaped up to run to better cover. One of the bullets hit him, and he fell into the pit. He wasn't dead, though, since he started yelling.

Cable came slithering over to Ketchum and handed him his cane. There was no sense in handing over the M16 he had slung over his shoulder beside the AR-15. They had nothing to fire at, although that didn't stop that damned Kale, probably imagining opposition all around them. He seemed determined to use up every scrap of ammo he had on him.

"Round up Buff," Ketchum told Cable. "We've got to get the hell out of here pronto."

Buff came crawling over on his belly across the mud.

"We gotta get outta here!" Ketchum yelled. "Right now. We'll go as light as we can."

Buff nodded toward the grenade launcher. "What about this?"

"Drop it! Let's go."

Once the three of them were together in a tight bunch, they took off, slowly and carefully, staying right behind Cable and leaving the other two behind. Ketchum noticed that Buff was the only one of them who looked back to where Kale was madly firing away. After a brief pause as he shoved in a fresh clip, he continued to shoot into the brightly lit rainy night.

Chapter Ten

Al's eyes snapped open. "I'm awake," he said.

Maury stood next to the bed with one hand extended to push at Al's shoulder. He held the pump shotgun in his other hand and wore a yellow rain slicker with the hood pulled up over his head, looking like Captain Ahab. Even in the dim illumination coming from the shell-shaped night-light over in the corner of the room, Al could see Maury's face was shiny, and he was dripping. Rain was drumming hard on the roof. A harsh rumble of loud thunder told him the storm was right on them.

As soon as Maury hurried out of the room, Fergie got out on her side of the bed, and they both started dressing in warm flannel shirts and jeans. Al pulled on his boots and headed out to get his rain gear.

Tanner got up slowly from his bed, where he'd been curled up in the corner, and came over to follow along.

"You're gonna have to stay here, good boy, and guard the house," Al said. "Okay? Stay!"

Tanner eased down and sat like the Sphinx, watching him.

Bonnie stood at the front door, which was slightly ajar. She held the 30-06 and kept a sharp eye out on the front of the house. "Maury's gone to watch out the back side," she said. "I've already called Victor Kahlon at his home. He's a bit of a grump, don't you know, when he's awakened at this hour and has to come out into the wet. But he said the cavalry is on its way."

As if in answer, the sound of sirens was approaching.

Al and Fergie stepped outside in their rain gear as three sheriff's department SUVs pulled up in front of the house. Bonnie stood in the open doorway, holding the rifle.

Three deputies clambered out of their vehicles, donning their white Stetsons covered with clear plastic sleeves to fend off the rain. They tugged on flak jackets and reached in to pull out shotguns. Each also carried a tactical EDC L2 flashlight, except Bob, who held a black metal three-banded Nightstick flashlight.

Al knew two of them, Bob and Sandel. Bob was a buzz-cut sergeant who was no stranger to donuts. He was the senior of them and had developed more pronounced jowls since the last time Al had seen him. Sandel was a corporal, lean and ginger haired, who everyone expected to climb briskly up the department ranks. The other deputy looked young enough to have barely begun shaving. But Al supposed everyone looked younger to someone at the age he was.

Sandel nodded toward Bonnie. "Has she shot anyone?"

"Not yet," Al said, "but the day's barely had a chance to get started. It's early times."

"Should we wait on Victor?" Bob asked.

"We'd best check to see what's in the spiderweb first. He can catch up," Al replied.

He and Fergie started off into woods, and the three deputies followed.

"Stay real close," Al advised. "The woods are alive with traps and snares of one kind or another."

"How'd that come to be?" Sandel squinted into the pouring rain at the saggy, wet limbs.

"Just one of the charms of living out here in the wilds."

They all moved closer and made a tight group. Al kept his flashlight in his pocket, since the deputies had their beams darting around as well as lighting the way ahead. Plus, he knew where most of the traps and pitfalls were.

The lights in the distance among the trees led the way, and soon, they could hear shouting.

"They're armed," Al said.

Bob slowed to jack a shell into his shotgun's chamber.

"There was a lot of shooting earlier, Maury told me. But it's quieted down. Not a peep or a pop in a while." Al pointed out a trip wire, and the others shied away from it.

As they came out into the patch of woods where the spotlights were lighting up the area like Las Vegas, they heard voices clearly above the pouring rain.

"Kale, you dumb shit. Get down here and help me outta here."

"Don't you think if I could go anywhere, I would have?"

Sandel raised the beam of his flashlight to focus on a man in a camo suit, hanging in the air by one ankle. In one bandaged hand, he tightly held a weapon.

"Drop the gun!" Bob yelled. "Or I shoot."

"It's empty."

"Drop it anyway."

Kale let go, and the HK416 plopped into the mud and piles of wet leaves. Bob went over and got it, checking to confirm it was empty.

"Hey, get me down from here!"

"Hold on to your horses." Sandel and the other two deputies eased up to the edge of the pit, which was a good ten feet deep with the bottom filling with water. "You got a gun?"

"Shoot 'em, Biff. Shoot 'em!" Kale yelled from where he hung like a Christmas ornament.

Al looked down and saw an AR-15 on the ground at the edge of the hole. A few yards farther away, someone had left behind a grenade launcher. He sure was glad that hadn't gotten a chance to be used against his home.

"Just a pistol!" Biff yelled.

"Throw it as far away from you as you can."

Biff pulled his handgun out with two fingers and tossed it into the muddy water across the bottom of the hole. He held the other hand against his side. "I'm shot, and I'm gonna need some help. That dumbass up there shot me while he was spraying the woods like a kid with a sparkler."

"You'll be surprised to hear this," Al said, "but I'm not particularly sympathetic."

"I don't give a shit about that. Just get me outta here. I need a amblance!"

"We're gonna need a ladder or something," Sandel said.

"I've got a rope ladder tucked away for just this sort of thing," Al said. "But if it was up to me, I'd throw both ends in."

VICTOR WAS JUST PULLING up to park his truck behind the other cruisers when Al, Fergie, and the three deputies came out of the woods into the open rain, leading their two prisoners. Victor knew Kale and Biff from their photos, but he'd never met them in person. Both were in handcuffs.

Biff was bent over at the waist, grimacing and clutching his crotch area. His shirt was off and had been tied around a wound.

"Gonna need an ambulance for this one." Sandel nodded toward Biff. "His buddy shot him and knocked him into a pit. The other one was hanging in the air from a snare."

"Dumbass." Biff glared at Kale.

Victor glanced at Al, who shrugged. "You've got two live ones to take home. I hope that makes Clayton sit up in his chair and grin."

"What happened to the other three?"

Fergie crossed her hands and made a flapping sign, like a butterfly taking off.

"Not any kind of sign of them, of where they came from or left to?" Victor asked.

Bonnie came up to the little group. She was wearing rubber boots and a clear rain slicker over her flannel shirt. "Yeah. I slogged up to the end of the lane and took a hard look around. There wasn't so much as a print or puddle to show they came in that way."

"I'm told you're a pretty good tracker," Victor said. "There was nothing?"

"Not unless you count a porcupine that had been run over so many times it's gonna have to be buried in a pizza box."

"Yep, they're sure gone but not forgotten," Al said. "Ran out and left their chums behind."

"One of those one-way loyalty things, eh? Maybe that'll encourage these two to do some talking."

"I'd be surprised."

"You never did say what Meat Jenkins and Dirty Fingernails Huff were up to during their visit out here," Victor said.

Al grinned. "No. No, I didn't."

Chapter Eleven

As soon as Ketchum, Cable, and Buff finished their long slog through the downpour and mud to at last get back inside their trailer, Buff started to go apeshit crazy. They had heard the approaching sirens as they had left the Quinn property, but Ketchum imagined the arriving deputies would play the logical card and be looking for a vehicle leaving the area, not three soaked-to-the-skin men in camo slinking across the back ends of the properties along the lake, one of them with a cane that sank into the mud, nearly spilling him at every other step.

"They got Biff and Kale. Biff and Kale. Biff and Kale!" Buff's voice boomed, and he started to kick big holes in the wooden paneling that covered one wall. A low row of mice holes already lined the floorboards, but his holes could have let far bigger creatures through.

"Knock it off!" Ketchum yelled. "We gotta live in here, at least for a few more days. Don't tear it apart." He was tugging off his soaked clothes and slamming them to the floor, not in the most cheerful mood either.

"What're we gonna do?" Buff moaned. "Are we gonna do anything?"

Cable leaned his long guns against a far wall.

Rain was still coming down hard and steady, drumming away on the metal roof. Ketchum glanced at the closest window, where rain spiders were running in panicked rivulets down the pane. At least the rain had cleared away any sign of their coming or going.

"Go outside, and knock down some trees or something," he said. "We're gonna need this shelter for a few more days."

"But they got Kale and Biff!"

"I know, and I'm gonna figure out a way to get 'em clear. Biff done the same for me, and it's likely he's in the same hospital." Ketchum made himself stoop to pick up his own clothes off the floor and hung them up to dry. They would have to go back out into the weather soon enough.

"But... But..." Buff was nearly to the point of giving himself hiccups.

His acting like a slobbering kid only pissed off Ketchum all the more. "Get yourself a beer, and chill. They'll just patch Biff up, like they done for me. Then we'll swoop in and scoop him up, like he done for me."

"And the bitch's bunch?"

"Trust me. Before this is over, I'm gonna set fire to all of them and roast marshmallows over their screaming, burning bodies." Ketchum hobbled over to his bed and tugged off a blanket to wrap around his shoulders.

Cable and Buff stayed in their wet clothes for the moment.

As Buff went to get a beer from the cooler, Cable and Ketchum moved to the trailer's dinette table. Ketchum leaned his cane against the wall where it would be handy and lowered himself into a seat. He and Cable leaned forward and put their heads closer together.

"It's not likely they'll be dumb enough to leave only one deputy outside Biff's hospital door this time," Cable said.

"No. It's probable we'll need some sort of diversion."

"I can think of a few things. Nothing so radical as blowing up one of the hospital's wings, then?"

"Maybe something a touch softer than that. Besides, it's probably going to have to be you going inside this time. I can hardly pull it off with a limp and this damn thing on my arm." Ketchum nodded down to his right arm. "This calls for someone with stealth, agility, and half a brain on his shoulders."

"So not him, then?" Cable pointed at Buff, whose head was tossed back as he chugged a beer.

"No, not him. He's handy enough to have around for some things but not this. He should come but not be on point."

AL HAD TANNER IN THE bathtub and was washing mud off the dog's legs. His bathroom break outside had exposed him to a world of mud now that the hammering rain had reduced to a slow, steady drizzle.

"You're going to clean up that tub, aren't you?" Fergie had come into the bathroom to stand over Al's shoulder and watch.

"I always do. Can you give me a hand here? I can lift him, and you look for grass burrs in his paws, or we can do it the other way around."

"You lift him first, and I'll look."

Tanner was an Australian shepherd who'd weighed fifty-six pounds when he got taped up at the vet's. He was also old enough that he'd been close to being euthanized when Al took him home from the rescue center. Tanner had been through nearly as many adventures and close calls as they had, and getting shot was only the latest such incident.

Al dried off the dog as best as he could and lifted Tanner so that his paws stuck out.

"Back paws are clear," Fergie said.

Tanner squirmed in Al's arms.

"Ah. Here are two in the left front paw." Fergie was at it a minute. "Got 'em." She switched to Tanner's right paw, worked a bit, and finally said, "I got two already here, but I think there are four more. We'd better switch."

Al put Tanner down, and he shook hard, throwing out a spray of water. Al winced, knowing that couldn't be the best thing for a fairly fresh wound.

He got up, and Fergie sat on the edge of the tub and lifted Tanner as he had done.

Al took the paw and reached in between the pads to pull at two burrs there. Tanner bent forward and licked Al's hand, seemingly glad to be getting rid of the burrs. The next two were tangled tightly in the fur at the edge of Tanner's paws. Al got up and brought over some scissors. After wrestling only a minute or two, he was able to cut the fur holding the burrs in place.

He nodded, and Fergie gently set Tanner down. The dog's tail was wagging furiously, and he pressed against Al's leg.

"Aw, it's just like Androcles and the lion," Fergie said. "When he pulled the thorn from the lion's paw, the beast later saved his life when he was thrown to the lions in the Colosseum."

"You think Tanner will save me someday when I'm thrown to the dogs?"

"Could be. Stranger things have happened."

"DO WE HAVE A LITTLE time before you take your watch?" Maury asked Bonnie.

"Have you been taking Viagra again?"

"You know that darn near killed me the last time."

"I doubt that would stop you. You just stay here and watch Little Al. Let the desire build a bit."

"Trust me. It's all the way built."

"Don't you know that absence makes the heart grow fonder?"

"Are you sure the phrase doesn't have *harder* in it somewhere?"

"Oh, you."

"Well, you just come back soon, and know that I'm gonna be harder than Chinese algebra."

"What is wrong with you?" She tilted her curly blond head at him. "You're in your sixties."

"That's the thing, my little dumpling. There are parts of me that don't know that."

Chapter Twelve

Victor Kahlon and two deputies in uniform stood outside the operating room's door while a surgeon and his crew were inside, patching up the hole in Boudreaux "Biff" Groton.

The bullet that hit Biff had done an in-and-out through his groin, nipping some of his intestines, and had to be quite painful. He was still swearing and grumbling while being prepped.

"Just an inch or two farther, and you'd be singing in a different section of the choir," the surgeon had told him.

"Yeah, yeah. Just patch me up enough to get me back up to butt-kicking strength," Biff said.

"Really? You want to mess with Al's bunch after this?" Victor asked.

"Yeah. But only after I kick the dumbass from our bunch who shot me, that dickhead Kale."

He'd still been cussing away as they put him under and wheeled him into the OR.

Footsteps came down the hallway with the authoritative click of someone who didn't care much about sleeping patients and was intent on making his approaching presence known.

Kahlon glanced down the hallway. Yep, it was the hospital's head administrator, Benton Callihan, flanked by two nurses, one of them the head floor nurse. He'd seen the nurse go for the phone when he and the two deputies arrived on her floor.

Callihan's tie wasn't tightly tied, and he hadn't taken time to shave, since they'd awakened him. His oval face was already tinged a bit pink, contrasting with the sparse white hair on his dome of a head.

He came up to stand with his face a foot away from Victor's. The two nurses with him were like bookends, one on either side. "I don't know what you have in mind here..."

"Before you get wound up enough to spin down the hall, let me tell you a couple of things. I'm not even going to mention the possibility of obstruction."

"For not mentioning it, you pretty well put it on the table."

Victor ignored that. "We are here to protect you and see that nothing happens. We could always leave, if that's what you really want, but then all responsibility for what happens here would be on your head."

"Just... Just what are we talking about here? All I know is what I've heard from my nurses and what happened last time." The shade of pink on Callihan's face had turned darker and was moving upward, past his white eyebrows.

"Men may be headed here, armed and dangerous ones who may have already murdered. The man in your OR is one of them."

"For heaven's sake."

"Which is why we're going to whisk him out of here the moment your surgeon is done with him. He can do his post-op convalescing safely locked in a county cell."

"These men you say are coming. Why not catch them before they get inside the hospital?"

"We aim to do that, if possible. But they're devious, and I have only so many men on this. The ones I'll leave in what would have been the recovery room are the second line of defense."

"It sounds more like a trap to me."

"Call it what you want. We're doing everything we can to corral this bunch."

"Well, why wasn't I informed?"

"Didn't you get a text message from the sheriff himself?"

Callihan whipped out his phone from his inside jacket pocket. "Oh. Oh. There it is. I see." He turned to glare at the head nurse.

She took half a step back. "How was I supposed to know what kind of phone messages you're getting?"

The three of them took off down the hallway, but they came back an hour and a half later just as one of the deputies at the door to the OR said, "I think they're bringing him out now."

The surgeon had worked as fast as he dared and must have let Callihan know when he was finishing.

When they wheeled Biff out the door, he was still unconscious, with his good hand handcuffed to the gurney on the opposite side from a previous shoulder injury that had also been freshly patched again.

"Let's go," Victor said.

They hurried the gurney toward the elevator. An ambulance waited below.

He'd asked Clayton if this was worth all the money and manpower, and the sheriff had said, "If the end result is to slow down the flash anger of road rage a few times, yes."

While waiting for the elevator door to open, he heard Callihan telling the head nurse, "Let's see about emptying some of the rooms around the recovery room."

"Where can we take the patients? We're nearly full."

"Find a place, any place, and make that stat."

BUFF GOT UP FROM WHERE he'd been moping on one end of the couch. He was headed for the cooler again when Ketchum said, "Put a cork in that for now. No more drinking. We're off to do something about Cable."

"What about Kale?"

"He's probably already in a cell at the county lockup. Don't forget he's the dumb shit who shot Biff and damn near did in the rest of us the way he was spraying bullets all over the place."

"I seen guys go off like that in combat," Cable said. "They snap under battle paranoia and see enemies everywhere. It's like a mirage."

"Well, he can cool his heels in a cell until we can figure out a way to spring him. In the meantime, we have a chance to rescue Biff, if we move fast and right now."

The rain was still hammering on the metal roof, and all three of them gave it a glance. Then Ketchum shrugged. At least the sheets of rain would be good cover.

He looked around at the inside of the trailer. The place was a real dump, and that was before Buff had added some holes to the decoration. The pale-blue interior paint was flaking on those walls not paneled in cheap veneer. The rug was dirty and had paths worn into it. The ceiling sagged in a couple of places. But it was as good a hideout as any, and the price was right: free. The electricity and water had been left on, so maybe it was someone's fishing shack. When Cable had scouted and found the place, there'd been no new tracks on the lane, and the insides had been covered in dust. They'd had the devil's own time cleaning away the dust and shaking out the sheets. If anyone came around trying to claim the place, they could deal with him then.

Ketchum was tired, aching, and brimming with frustration at how the evening had gone. He could easily lie down and rest, as dingy as the place was.

He took a deep breath and used his cane to get up. "Let's do this."

Keep pushing, he told himself. *Push, push, push.*

Ketchum struggled back into his still slightly damp clothes, no easy task with a bum leg and a hand in a cast. But he neither asked for nor got any help from the other two.

He put his gun under his belt where he could get at it and wished he weren't wearing a cast on his shooting arm and that his leg didn't throb with every step. *But I could wish in one hand and... Oh well. It's time to do this.* "Come on. We need to get a hustle on."

Cable stripped off his wet camo outfit and went to the closet to take out the only scrap of clothing left in the place, a silver-and-black Bass Pro Shop jacket with the lining worn out. It wouldn't stop the rain worth a whoop, nor would it keep him warm, but he slipped it on anyway.

Ketchum drove. The wiper on his side wasn't the best, but he could see, barely, and he drove as slowly as he dared, given their hurry. On the way to the hospital, he pulled over long enough for Cable to hop out and switch out the truck's license plates with ones they'd gotten from some unfortunate dude who might soon get pulled over for a stolen-car check. But it would probably be hours before he woke to enjoy that treat. It would buy their truck some time.

At one point in the downpour, a cop car pulled out with its red and blue lights flashing. It pulled right up behind Ketchum, whose stomach clenched. But the cruiser went around to his left and chased some other hapless sucker whose bad night was just beginning.

When he got to the hospital, he drove around it a couple of times and finally found a parking spot where the truck could point out and be ready for a quick getaway. A hospital at night and in the rain was a somber sight, full of worries and woe along with a night-shift staff getting by on sips of coffee while their family members were home in their cozy beds. Biff had told him how he'd slipped into the place through an employee entrance to steal a white coat at a locker room.

Ketchum wasn't sure which door that was. He wished he could ask Biff, but that was out of the question. He glanced left and couldn't believe his luck. Someone's sweetheart ride, a green 1957 Chevy station wagon that looked in mint condition, had a white coat hanging in the window of the backseat.

"Buff?" He nodded toward it. "We need a white coat for Cable."

The car was from a pre-car-alarm era, unless someone had installed one, which he doubted. It probably belonged to some doctor or well-off nurse and wouldn't be all that hard to steal, but it would be too conspicuous and easy to spot. Besides, they were truck sort of guys.

Buff eased his bulk out into the rain, went over to the car, looked around, and slammed his elbow into the back window, which shattered in sparkles of glass that mixed with the rain as they fell. He grabbed the white coat, got back in the car, and handed the coat up to Cable.

"I'd wait until you're inside before you put it on, or you'll be a dripping mess."

Cable nodded. He rolled up the white coat and slipped it inside his jacket. Without a pause, he opened the passenger door and took off at a bent-over run toward the nearest hospital door.

A DEPUTY WAS POSTED just inside the door. Cable waited until he went to look around a corner. When he disappeared, Cable opened the door and dashed inside.

All was clear where he stood, in a foyer with a few plants and chairs for waiting. A receptionist behind a desk fifty feet down the hall was talking into her headset and looking away. At that late hour, the expectation of visitors had to be low.

Cable tugged on the white coat and walked briskly the other way, toward an elevator. He wished he had a stethoscope like he'd used in the service to hang around his neck. But as he passed a bulletin board, he saw a clipboard hanging at the bottom with some sort of sign-up sheet on it. He grabbed it. A clipboard always lent an official sort of look to anyone.

Ketchum had told him what floor to check, where he'd been before Biff came to his rescue. He took the elevator up to that floor. The ping as the door opened seemed excessively loud, but that was because he was trying to be soundless.

He stepped out into the hallway and saw no one in either direction. So far, it had been easy. *Too easy?* He started checking room numbers, and the rooms he passed were empty. The closed swinging doors at the end of the hall had two small windows with chicken wire inside the panes. A female face popped up, saw him, and popped back down. She wore a nurse's white cap. He expected her to come through the door to talk to him. Instead, the door stayed shut.

Uh-oh. Something hinky was going on, and he didn't intend to linger and find out what it was.

The elevator pinged again as the doors opened. A sleeve that looked like it belonged to a deputy sheriff appeared.

Without any hesitation, he pushed open the door to the stairwell beside him and clambered down the stairs. He didn't slow or pause until he was at the floor where he had come in. Dashing across the foyer, he tugged off his white coat, and he dropped it as soon as he was going out the door. A shout came from behind him as well as pounding footsteps. They sounded like they were made by the sort of duty boots deputy sheriffs wore.

His fears were confirmed as a uniformed deputy burst out the door he had just exited. "Stop!"

Cable had no intention of stopping or even slowing. He went around a corner of the brick building and could see Ketchum's truck waiting. The deputy behind him had quit yelling and was gaining on him.

Just as the deputy shot around the corner, a bulky figure stepped from the shadows and held an arm straight out. The deputy ran into the stiff arm with his throat, clotheslining himself, and dropped to the ground. He was gagging, struggling to breathe when Buff stepped closer and put his full weight behind a punch to the deputy's temple.

When Cable looked back, Buff was smiling as he jogged along. The deputy lay stretched out on the sidewalk like a doormat. Neither tried to speak, just ran as fast as they could go to climb into the truck.

Ketchum took off while they were still closing the doors but made no screech of tires, just accelerated until they were zipping along and soon out of sight of the hospital.

"You're not gonna ask how it went?" Cable asked.

"No need. We didn't spring him free, but at least we didn't lose anyone else."

"Now what?"

"There's always a plan C and maybe even a plan D."

Chapter Thirteen

Victor had barely started his truck down Al's lane when once again he had to pull far to the side, into some low brush, to let a flatbed truck carrying a backhoe through.

After the truck had passed, he saw Al and his sidekicks, Dirty Fingernails Huff and Meat Jenkins, coming out of the woods, carrying the gear they had used to rig booby traps throughout the woods.

Al came up to the open driver's-side window of the truck.

"Why are you taking down your defense system?" Victor asked. "I gather you filled in all the pits as well."

"I didn't want any of the deer and other critters of the woods harmed. You'll remember I fed and watered the deer and got them through that longish drought we had from 2011 to 2015."

"Don't you think those human varmints might come through the woods once they figure out you've removed all the traps?"

"I figure it's like Mark Twain said about a cat that sat on a hot furnace once. Not only would it no longer sit on a hot furnace, it wouldn't sit on any furnace."

Victor shook his head, waiting.

"I guess you came out here to tell me Clayton isn't happy with the two we caught," Al said.

"That's right. Kale and Biff won't make the road rage statement Clayton wants. Besides, neither of them is talking. They've both reduced to giving name, rank, and serial number, like this is war."

"It kind of is." Al looked over to where Huff and Meat were starting up the lane toward the house, carrying the snare materials. When he looked back at Victor, he said, "You know, everything isn't always about what Clayton wants."

"You know what it's like if you work for him."

Al nodded.

"This sort of sustained rage isn't as unusual as it should be. Texas has had its share of feuds, ones that would put that Hatfield-McCoy scuffle to shame. Hate is being fueled by politicians, extreme groups, and the usual handful of zealots no one should listen to, but some do."

"You haven't been able to pin anything on them about the armory job?"

"That was in another county, and their forensics folks are far in the shadow of ours."

"How about blowing up Heck Marmon's place?"

"You know how little was left after that. Diddly-squat. All we got were tire tracks tracing to a stolen truck that was detailed so clean you could eat off any surface when we found it."

"Bonnie saw all of them here, attacking us. Hell, I saw them. The two you have were armed while caught trespassing on my land."

"Sure, we have them for that. That gives us enough to hang on to them. But that doesn't give us what Clayton was after, something to shift the focus to that road rage incident involving Bonnie. The two we have are staying as silent as deep-water clams. Haven't even threatened to lawyer up. It's like they think Ketchum will figure out a way to bust them out or spring them free."

"So it's Ketchum Clayton needs. Nothing else will do?"

"The good news, bad news there is that he's out there somewhere and just as prone to violence and anger as ever. But Clayton wants him alive."

"All I know is that Ketchum's lot has set their hats for Bonnie and anyone around her. She's family, and I think you know what that means."

"Indeed, I do," Victor said.

In the rearview mirror, Victor saw someone walking down the lane toward them. When she got closer, he could see it was Bonnie. She was carrying a 30-06 and had a box of ammo sticking out of her jeans pocket.

"See anything up on the road?" Al asked.

"Just a bunch of them black chickens havin' a memorial service over a raccoon who wasn't as fast as he thought he was. They're doing what they can to keep him from being just another biological speed bump."

"Why don't you take a rest?" Al suggested.

"Naw, I'm gonna spell Maury, who's been watching the shore side."

As she walked away, Victor asked, "Doesn't she know she's the number-one target of these guys?"

"Oh, she knows. I'm just trying to figure out if she kind of enjoys that."

CABLE WATCHED KETCHUM closely. The man was like a time bomb. *Tick. Tick. Tick.* They were supposed to be resting, carefully thinking things over, and figuring out what to do next. Ketchum's face was gradually growing redder and redder. There didn't look to be a shred of care or logic there, just pure raw bile and hate iced over with a layer of anger.

Suddenly, Ketchum leaped to his feet, if pushing himself up from his seat with the help of a cane counted as leaping. At the least, he got up swiftly. "Let's do something!"

"What?"

"Anything."

"We could steal a boat again," Cable said. "They probably don't expect that."

"Make it happen," Ketchum said. The fire in his belly was like one of those fierce Texas grass fires that left huge patches of prickly pear cactus looking like twisted black pieces of licorice. He went over to the wall and picked up the M16 leaning there. He had to prop himself up against the wall while he checked the gun's action, not for the first time.

Cable slipped out the trailer's door and went down the steps to stand and take deep breaths. He'd thought it best to get out of there before Ketchum started shooting all over the place the way Kale had done, damn any collateral damage.

He went down to the lake's shore and thought for a few minutes. He'd looked over the marinas of the nearest property owners' association. They were locked with chain-link gates with those panels where you couldn't slip around the side, and they were lit up like Las Vegas with security lights everywhere and cameras, so slipping up to the gate with bolt cutters wasn't a terrific idea. He'd found out the cheapest slips they offered were two hundred fifty dollars a month, and you had to get on a list and wait for someone to die before you could berth your boat there. Hence the security.

Cable's best chances were to scout along the shoreline and hope to get lucky. He flipped a mental coin and took off to his left. A distant rumble in the darkening sky hinted that it wasn't the best day to be on the water. He could make out only a couple of boats towing water-skiers and a few Jet Skis being zipped around by crazies who looked like they were trying to upset themselves.

The first couple of lots near the trailer were rough going, unde-veloped shorelines with chaparral grown thick and thorny with yucca, mesquite, prickly pear cacti, poison oak, locust, and just about every-thing else out to stick Cable through his Levi's. He picked his way through with care and still felt a stab or two before he came out onto a more manicured lawn.

He had to be even more careful, since he was out in the open and could see up the steep slope of the lawn that led up to a near-mini man-sion of a house. Cable stayed as close to the water as he could and eased his way to the boat house, which had a slide and a swing that would take someone out over the water. But the boat house was empty, the boat perhaps in dry dock somewhere, getting tuned up for better times.

Each of the next several houses stood up on the same cliff, so the ones with boat houses had long, sometimes winding paths up to the house. The boat houses themselves were usually mounted on rail systems so they could be lowered or raised depending on the water level. Lake Travis was usually six hundred eighty-one feet above sea level when full, but the surface level could flex by as much as fifty or more feet. Droughts and heavy water use by citizens in Austin led to the lower levels, with gushes of hard rain coming from a wide watershed accounting for the level rising.

The next few boat houses he searched had boats locked and secured. Not until he got to a slightly more worn open boat house beneath what looked more like a cabin on the upper end of the slope did he get lucky. Inside the shed, hanging on the two straps of an electric winch, was something that would do very well, an aluminum Ranger Deep-V-series bass boat, with an electric motor mounting on the bow and with a Mercury Pro XS motor, a five-hundred-pound powerhouse that would push the light aluminum boat across the water with its two hundred fifty horsepower as fast as he could want. The craft was seventeen feet long and had enough room to handle Buff being aboard. The V hull would mean it was quieter on the water when at rest and wouldn't have the water from wakes thumping at its sides as loudly as a tri-hull would.

He kept an eye on the distant cabin as he slipped into the boat. Easing into the console on the right side, he reached and felt under the dash. *A-ha!* His fingers closed on a key and rubber float hanging from a hook far inside. He took it out, inserted it, checked the gas level, which was half full, and glanced up at the house. After springing out, he went over and hit the switch that lowered the boat. As soon as it was bobbing in the water well above the lifting straps, he got in and used a small emergency oar to push the boat free from its berth. The wind and current saved him work as the boat drifted easily along the shore until he was nearly out of sight of the cabin. He turned the key, and the motor gave a hearty rumble. Cable pushed the lever forward gradually, giving it more gas. He made a wide, sweeping turn and headed back toward the trailer. *We have ourselves a boat.*

When he eased the boat to the shore below the trailer, Ketchum and Buff were standing by the tattered half remains of the wooden dock. Ketchum was leaning on his cane, while Buff carried two of the AR-15s and the M16 Ketchum had claimed as his. They had brought along the case of grenades. Ketchum had the Korth pistol he had acquired shoved under his belt at the front, while all Cable had was his belt knife.

"What took so long?" Ketchum snapped.

They gingerly crossed what was left of the dock. Ketchum gestured for Cable to slide over, that he would drive. After Buff got the guns and the box of grenades onto the deck by the back seats, he helped Ketchum down into the boat. They were barely settled when Ketchum swung the boat out into the deeper water and went back up along the way to a house they all knew too well.

As they started off, Cable looked at the sky, which was dark with flashes of light and thunder coming from the even-darker horizon. *Helluva time to be boating.* Cable figured they had an hour or so before the day got uglier.

While they were still three hundred yards from their target, Ketchum turned the key, killing the engine. He jerked his head toward the bow.

Cable climbed onto the bow and lowered the electric motor into the water. He sat in the small raised fishing seat and used the foot pedal to turn the boat toward the Quinn place. The plus side was that the boat moved quietly along, and they might just look like fishermen out on the lake. On the downside, he was sitting high in an open place, should anything sudden and peppy happen, as it had before with those people.

Buff handed the M16 up to Ketchum, who held it across his lap. With both hands free, he could shoot from where he sat. His eyes were narrow slits as he stared ahead at the approaching shore, boat house, and fishing dock where they were headed.

Cable kept a sharp eye on the shore and all the way up the concrete steps to the house. He thought he heard a metallic sound he recognized and looked back at Ketchum, but his gun was still across his lap. His mind clicked rapidly through possibilities until he landed on a shell being jacked into the chamber of a bolt-action rifle.

Before he could yell, "Watch out!" a shot came at them from the shore. Then another and another, as fast as the bolt could be worked and the trigger pulled.

He heard and felt loud thumps beneath his feet, tearing holes into the aluminum hull.

"Get down, everyone!" Ketchum yelled.

Cable was way ahead of him and had dived to sprawl across the bow.

"She's not shooting at us. That bitch! She's shooting at the boat!" Cable shouted. "And she's hitting it right where she wants to!"

As he said it, a round punched through and hit right between Ketchum's legs. Another hit the electric motor and shattered it. The sound of it stopped abruptly.

Cable felt the bow lowering. They were taking on water. She had already punched a hole in the bow as big as a tennis ball, maybe bigger.

"Get shooting, you guys." Ketchum raised the M16.

"We're sinking, you fool!" Cable yelled. "We've got to run for it."

Ketchum glared, and his eyes threw sparks at Cable. But as the boat lowered farther, he set aside the M16 and turned on the boat's big gas motor. He swung out toward deeper water and opened the throttle.

The boat rose and settled into a plane, but water was still rushing in, even harder with the speed.

They had only gone a couple of miles before the water was to their knees, and the boat was settling deeper by the second. Ketchum steered the boat until they were gradually closer to shore.

"We're sinking!" Buff shouted, not missing an opportunity to state the obvious.

Water was splashing onto Cable and had nearly filled the insides of the aluminum boat.

Ketchum missed a real opportunity to be Captain Ahab and yell, "Abandon ship!" Instead, he just quietly took the Korth from under his belt, left it on his seat, climbed awkwardly over the side, plopped into the water, and started swimming for the shore, which was fortunately only twenty yards away.

Cable slid into the cool water and started swimming as well, no easy feat with all his clothes and boots on, but damned if he was going to kick off his boots. He'd drown first. As he swam, he thought of the long guns, the case of grenades, and the pistols back in the boat. All were doing their part along with the five-hundred-pound motor to help the boat sink. Probably the smarter thing to have done would have been to steer closer to shore earlier and get off while they were still able to walk to the house. But that woman had been shooting away and hadn't missed a thing yet.

Buff came splashing along beside him. Ketchum, who was struggling to stay afloat and could only kick with one leg, grabbed onto Buff. The big guy headed for a private boat house, even though Cable could see people on its dock. Ketchum was dragged along. Cable swam hard to keep up.

At the dock, Buff started up the ladder, reaching back to pull Ketchum onto it too. From the deck of the boat house, a man shouted, "What are you guys up to?"

"Our boat sank out there!" Ketchum yelled back. He was struggling to stay as polite as possible, though Cable knew he had to be really steaming inside by then. Cable was damn sure he wouldn't bring up what they might have done differently when they were alone.

"Oh. Okay, then." The man had white hair and wore a fishing shirt over his jeans. "You're sure going to need some dry clothes. You're soaked to the skin, and that water can't be very warm."

"It isn't," Ketchum said. "But we'll just be on our way."

"Are you sure you don't want—?"

"We'll be on our way." His voice was sterner the second time. He put an arm around Buff, who reached down to help keep him up, since he'd lost his cane. They started to slog up the slope, heading for the road beyond.

The woman, whose hair was as white as her husband's, rolled her eyes at Cable as he went dripping behind them.

Once around the house, a good-sized one done in golden stucco with two pools out back connected by a small waterfall, they started up the paved drive toward the road.

Halfway there, Buff said, "Hold him up a minute," handing Ketchum over to Cable.

Buff went over to a sapling peach tree supported by ropes going down to pegs in the ground. He broke off the top of the tree, tossed that aside, then broke off the two-inch-thick trunk near the ground. Then he came back and handed the five-foot length to Ketchum to use as a temporary cane.

Ketchum took it without a word of thanks. They continued up the lane.

Cable thought there might be a moment when Ketchum would say something about all their guns and grenades, which might well be at the bottom of the deep already. But he didn't. He just glared straight ahead as they got to the end of the lane and turned in the direction of the trailer, still with a long ways to go.

Chapter Fourteen

Victor Kahlon called back twenty minutes after Al put in a call to the sheriff's department, asking to talk with him as soon as possible.

"What's the big rush? I'm over here on the far side in the butthole of the county."

"That's good to know," Al said.

"Why's that?"

"That means where I'm standing isn't the butthole of the county."

"I can arrange for the title change if you don't have something good for me."

"I do. It's a lead."

"Okay. You have my interest." Kahlon's voice went all business, like the crack of a whip. "What've you got?"

"Can you check to see if anyone's fishing boat with a blue hull and Mercury motor has been stolen?"

"I can. Why?"

"The remaining few of those RKs were just in it and were coming toward our house."

"How did that turn out? I'm guessing not well for them, since you're alive and on the phone."

"The boat sprang a leak. Bonnie was watching the shore and had the 30-06."

"You're all okay?"

"Just dandy."

"Any casualties for them?"

"No. We were abiding by Clayton's wish to get his hands on Ketchum while he's alive."

"She didn't clip any of their tail feathers, did she?"

"They were all alive, unharmed, and well when they left here, only they were in somewhat of a hurry, since the boat was getting lower in the water as they went."

"I can imagine that, with Bonnie shooting. But if they'd have kept coming..."

Al said nothing.

"Well, you know what Clayton wants."

"And he knows the Rubicon these guys are seeking to cross," Al said. "You know I don't operate out of anger. I do what needs to be done. If those guys push too hard, though, I'm going to pin them like butterflies to a board."

"I'll let Clayton know you're playing along as best you can. And I'll get back to you about the fishing boat with a blue hull and a Mercury motor."

Half an hour later, Al was walking back toward the house along the lane after having a look around on that end when Victor called back. Fergie was watching the lakeside, while Maury and Bonnie were savoring a family and rest time with Little Al.

This is one helluva way to live, Al thought as he reached for his phone. *Having to watch our backs, not being able to live normal lives, all because some complete asshole has an imagined agenda and is just wacky enough to act on it.*

Almost every one of the drivers of trucks and cars that had gone by while he was out by the road had waved at him, like it was a normal, everyday world going on out there, and a mostly friendly one.

"Please tell me you have these dirtbags in custody," Al said before Victor could get a word out.

"I wish. The boat hasn't been reported as missing. The owners may be gone or at the least don't even know it was taken yet. So we have no starting point there."

"You've got nothing at all to go on?"

"Actually, the trail just gets wispier," Victor said. "Some folks in the department are making side bets that these jaspers have skedaddled, headed for parts unknown."

"Not these guys." Al heard a rustle and lowered the phone. A lizard scurried across dried leaves, slapping alternate limbs to the ground as it waddled in a rush to tuck itself under a rock pressed against the trunk of a tree. "How about pickup trucks?" he asked when he put the phone back up to his ear.

"We're way ahead of you on that one. We've checked out every stolen vehicle, keeping a special eye out for trucks, since one was used at the armory. There were quite a number of thefts to sort through, but a handful fit with how these guys might have worked. Some stolen ones were found near where others disappeared, and the plates were often switched around. But whoever among them is doing the detail work is a crackerjack, because we haven't found a print or hint of DNA, even in the most unlikely places."

Al shook his head, though he doubted Victor heard any rattle over the phone. "As badly shot up as that boat was, and with a heavy motor and who knows what else was on board in the way of weapons, it's probably not going to be found on the surface anywhere."

"I can hardly send out divers. Visibility underwater is pretty bad. The lake's especially murky after that last rain. That's if we even knew where to start."

"I guess you're doing all you can."

"Al, everyone here knows it's you in the middle right now. They all support you, and they have Clayton pushing them like a stagecoach driver with a whip, so yeah, we're doing all that manpower and time allow while handling the usual full plate of other stuff."

CABLE AND THE OTHER two were tired. They were wet, and they had just slogged all the way back to their stupid dank trailer. All Cable wanted to do was lie down and take a nap. But as they hiked the last few feet up to their stolen truck and the trailer, Cable took one look at Ketchum and knew that wasn't going to happen.

Ketchum's eyes were red rimmed and looked a little swollen. He stabbed the ground with his supportive rod and stared blankly ahead. That was the look of a madman. Pity the poor giant white whale to come swimming across his harpoon-holding path.

Cable fancied he could read the nuances of people as readily as he could fathom the hidden messages of the woods and trails. They were all tired. Buff was dragging his wagon and looked ready to sleep where he stood. But they would go on. Why? Because Ketchum led them. Cable would follow too. *It's rare in life you find someone as full of purpose and as driven, even if the fuel is hate.*

Ketchum mumbled, perhaps trying to communicate with them but more likely just on his own wavelength. "You know they got all kinds a names like 'homo-phone-bic' and 'miss-something-phone-bic.' Fact is people just piss me off."

"Except us?" Buff asked.

Ketchum squinted in his direction, no human warmth in his eyes. "Yeah, except you guys."

There was no conviction or shred of truth in his voice. Yet they followed him. Ketchum had practically recruited Cable for his woodsy skills and Buff for the fact that he was large and in charge when it came to thumping on anyone.

"What do we do now?" Buff asked.

"I know a guy," Ketchum said, turning to Cable, his face haggard, a bit of drool at the corner of his mouth. "A guy with his share of guns,

who might just be willing to part with them with the proper encour-
agement."

Chapter Fifteen

Ketchum eased their current truck, a dark-blue crew-cab GMC Canyon with four-wheel drive, into a thick stand of pecan trees, each with a trunk more than four feet wide.

"These trees were around when the Injuns rode the hills 'round here," Cable said.

Ketchum didn't care a whoop about that. He was just glad for a place where the surrounding brush and thick trunks hid the truck. "Why don't you get out and have a look around?"

Cable nodded. He got out slowly and closed the passenger-side door carefully. It barely made a click as it snicked shut. Before heading back toward the house, he went back to the road and wiped out any sign of their tire tracks.

Buff had already eased his head back. His mouth hung open as he took deep breaths, already asleep.

Ketchum could use a few winks himself. His body was exhausted, but his mind was whirring like a buzz saw gone mad. Still, it seemed he had hardly closed his eyes for a second when he was awakened by Cable climbing back into the truck.

"He's back there. How long do we wait?"

"As long as we hafta. Everyone leaves sometime."

The crew-cab truck was the right size for working outfits to travel together for construction, ranch work, or whatever. It was also right for stretching a bit and catching up on much-needed sleep. Ketchum soon nodded off again.

He woke to Cable shaking his shoulder, fortunately not the wounded one. "I heard a truck go past. Let's say we go have a look at the house."

Ketchum started the engine while Cable reached back to rouse Buff, who at first was as grumpy as a bear rattled out of hibernation.

Harley Combers, the man who lived in the house set way back from the road and in its own thick woods, was someone they had met at the shooting range as well. He was a big black man, almost as big as Buff. He'd told them he'd just gotten divorced but that he missed her very much. He'd broken into tears as he told how his wife left him for a barista ten years younger than her, and he had yanked out a big blue bandana to daub at his eyes. Ketchum thought that made the guy look vulnerable, which knocked him down a notch or two in his estimation.

"Just because you knock her head around the house a time or two like a handball, she shouldn't up and leave you," Harley had said. He was a pretty fair shot and usually had a variety of new and different guns with him. Ketchum might have considered him to join them, but there was that crying, and for Pete's sake, the man was black.

After Ketchum pulled up a ways short of the house, Cable slipped on ahead but soon came out the front door and gave a thumbs-up.

Ketchum was thinking about that round blond bitch and her bunch as he climbed out of the driver's seat, muttering, "These guys are forcing us into a life of crime."

Buff threw a rock through the back door but didn't trip a booby trap. When Ketchum and Cable poured inside, covering every corner with their guns, they found the place as empty as their hopes and dreams. But they did find something.

"Oh my laws," Ketchum said.

He stepped into a side room, a former guest bedroom perhaps, that was a wonderland. Harley had bragged that he had been to a gun show or two, and he'd taken some pretty righteous stuff out to the shooting range, but Ketchum had no idea the man had loaded up on as much as he was seeing before him. He could imagine why a wife might not admire a room like this, especially since all the appliances in the house were old and worn, but it was heaven in their eyes. Even though the gun safe was closed, the rack that ran along the far wall held more weapons than Ketchum had ever seen outside a gun store. Boxes of ammo for each gun were lined along the base of the rack, while more ammo filled the shelves on either side of the room's only window, which had been sealed with a grating of iron bars.

Before the others could call dibs, he rushed to scoop the HK416 off the rack and cradle it in his arms. It was the same sort of gun Kale had been so smitten with and misused, a special forces and Delta Force dream gun. It sat next to a couple of the usual AK-47s, one of the newer AK-100s, and an Uzi that Harley had fired at the range a couple of times, although Ketchum wouldn't take one if it was given to him. But the HK416 was going to make some happy music for him.

He passed over a couple of Israeli models, the IMI Galil and the Tavor TAR-21. Though he'd heard good things about how well-trained and well-armed the Mossad were, and he had heard nothing against the Israel Defense Forces, he'd never fired either gun. Both weapons looked like they needed a learning curve, and he doubted they'd match the ammo that would work best for all of them. Plus, he had to admit to himself he was more than a little anti-Semitic.

Buff and Cable each selected an AR-15, something each could readily use, although Cable teetered for a moment or two over a SIG SG 550, the standard issue for the Swiss army, although why Switzerland had an army in the first place was beyond Ketchum, since the damned place was neutral in any war that mattered. Among the pistols, Ketchum found a Colt Python, which he took as his sidearm. He still missed his stolen Korth like a son. Hard to believe something so expensive was at the bottom of the lake and was soon going to rust and rot away into nothing.

Cable kept slipping over to the front of the house to peek outside. He pulled aside a ruffled pink drape from one of the front windows and said, "Heads up. He's back. He just dropped a twelve-pack of Coors and is reaching back into the truck. Now he's back out, armed, and coming in hot."

Ketchum had already jammed a banana clip into the Heckler & Koch. He let his cane drop and hobbled over to one of the front windows, using the weapon as his cane.

By the time Harley was halfway to the door, they all had loaded weapons ready.

"On three," Ketchum said. "One... two... three!"

They smashed out the lower panes of each window with the barrels of their guns and opened fire before the bits of falling glass had hit the ground.

Harley started to raise his gun the second he heard the noise, but they were already firing away. His body jerked more than a dozen times, his weapon falling, and he crumpled on top of it.

"Nice of him to bring us beer," Buff said.

"And there's always a certain satisfaction to shooting anyone with his own guns," Cable said.

Buff set about loading the weapons and ammo they'd selected into the truck and grabbed the twelve-pack of Coors. Cable found a can of gas in the wooden shed that housed tools. He started toward the house with it.

"Hold off on that." Ketchum stood over Harley's fallen remains, not to say a few words but to figure out what was best. "Let's not do it the same. We'll be starting to leave a pattern."

"What, then?"

"Bury him."

Cable kicked a heel into the dirt. "Ground's kinda hard."

"It'll be softer over in those woods. Plus, if we need more stuff, we might be able to come back here and shop some more, 'less someone who might miss ol' Harley here comes around."

Sighing, Cable headed toward the toolshed. "C'mon, Buff, and fetch that wheelbarrow leaning against that tree. No reason we have to carry this lump o' flesh."

Ketchum leaned on his cane and watched. He was tired to the very aching core of his bones. But it had been a good and productive day, and he planned to sleep well and hard.

Chapter Sixteen

Lieutenant Luke Chandler got out of his Austin PD cruiser, came over to Victor's truck, where the passenger door was open, and slid in.

Victor's heart beat a little faster, adrenaline already pumping out to the ends of his toes and fingers. It would be a real coup for him if he could collar those guys, not to mention a major relief to Al Quinn and therefore Sheriff Clayton, who thought of his retired department detective as a son.

He pulled out, and the big, square green SWAT truck holding the sheriff's department tactical force eased onto the road behind him. Chandler had cooperated before with the department's auto-theft task force and had once trained under Fergie. His call had mobilized the effort and gave him the right to tag along.

"If these turn out to be the ones I'm after, they are armed and should be considered volatile and dangerous." Victor glanced over at Chandler. "But if at all possible, Clayton would like to capture them alive."

"Humph."

"We suspect them for a couple of murders as well. How did you tumble to this location?"

Chandler was looking out his window, watching the green of the countryside go by. Most of his driving in Austin must have covered streets and back alleys. The nature part of the drive might be a treat for him, Victor figured.

"The vehicle-theft part of the MO matched what you were seeing, often leaving the last stolen vehicle where the new one was copped. We got lucky, and someone spotted one of the recently stolen trucks go by out in your turf. He saw where they went but stayed back. Our lead came from an overenthusiastic citizen called Pipple Landry. Kind of a pain in the ass usually. The kind of guy who listens to police-band radios and likes to feel he's helping. This time, he might just have. The unit you sent to take a peek at the place said there were people there, and they shouldn't be. The owner's over in The Woodlands, part of Houston."

They were getting closer, and Victor's pulse beat faster. "So just vehicle theft? That's what you were after this bunch for?"

"No. We think they're active juggers as well. They've hurt some people but no murders."

Chandler didn't have to explain jugging. A crew hung out around an ATM or a bank, saw someone come away with money, and swooped in while the victim was fiddling with car keys or a cell phone. Sometimes, they even waited until the victims got home and robbed them in their own driveways.

"That's where we got a glimpse of one license plate," Chandler said, "from a door video."

"Let's hope these are the guys I'm after."

"Not to rain on your parade, but I hope these are my guys, the juggers." Chandler grinned.

They got to the right lane, and Victor pulled onto the shoulder to let the SWAT-team truck lead the way. Then he pulled out and followed. As they went around a bend in the wooded lane, a truck was parked in front of a trailer.

Victor and Chandler got out and stood far enough away that they could see and not get in the way or present themselves as targets.

"You said the guys you're after have guns but haven't used them yet," Victor said.

"If you don't count a little pistol whipping, no. But they're a rough-and-tumble-looking group of black men in their thirties, all with past records, and I think they're apt to feel the wall against their backs and do almost anything."

The sheriff's department tactical team's leader, Jeb Martindale, held up a hand, and the men in their gear deployed to the back and front of the house. Three with the heavy steel ram stood by the door. Jeb raised his hand again then lowered it abruptly. *Wham!* The ram swung out and back, crashing into the door.

Almost at once, gunfire sounded above the shouting. Victor shook his head. That wasn't what he'd wanted or at least what Clayton wanted.

The flurry of shots lasted less than a minute. Glass flew out of one front window then the other, shreds of the formerly closed venetian blinds slipping out of the holes along with broken crystal shards.

Chandler glanced at Victor, who shrugged.

Abruptly, the shooting stopped. Jeb came out the front door, looked at them, and shook his head. He was talking to someone on his chest mic as they went by to have a look inside. Victor heard the words "had no choice" and figured Jeb was preparing for an unhappy talk with Clayton.

Some of the SWAT team headed out the back door, while the others took a look at the bodies. Victor's heart dipped.

The men who had unwisely fired at the SWAT team were all black and in their thirties, though their faces and hands showed hard wear. Four of them had their shirts off, while the other two wore grimy white T-shirts. One of them groaned. Three were being cuffed, while the others didn't need cuffs. An ambulance would already be on the way for those who'd been wounded.

Victor looked around at the men of the SWAT team.

One of them said, "We're all fine. Them, not so much."

Victor thought he heard a Jamaican accent in the mumblings of one of the injured men, while another had a drawn-out Texas drawl.

"These the guys you were after?" Victor asked.

Chandler nodded.

"Your boss didn't specifically say to try to take them alive, did he?"

"No. But we always try."

Jeb came over to Victor. "Not a single one of our guys got hurt. That's a wonder. Do you think Clayton's gonna be pissed?"

"I doubt it. You and your men did a good job."

As Victor and Chandler went out the front door, he thought about Al. *This isn't going to be good news for him.*

It would be a while before they heard sirens from the ambulances. Victor listened to the woods around them settling down. Birds began to twitter once again, and the upper limbs of trees swayed and rustled in the breeze. All peaceful enough for the moment, but that didn't let Victor's stomach settle back down. The men he was after were still out there somewhere. He had half a dozen other cases on his plate, but that bunch gnawed at him.

Chapter Seventeen

Buff crossed the room and looked into the bedroom, where Ketchum was still sleeping and snoring hard enough to rattle the trailer's eaves.

"You'd better let him sleep," Cable said. "We can take some kind of action when he wakes up. He needs to sleep right now, catch up, or he's gonna be seven ways boone-dog crazy."

Buff looked back at Cable. "Yeah, he's a bit there already."

"Sure enough."

"But don't you think he's gonna be mad when he wakes up?"

"Hell, mad is his favorite color."

Buff went over to the cooler and found two slices of bologna and an open can of pickled jalapeños. There were two slices of white bread left with little green spots speckled across them. "Want to split a sandwich?"

Cable shook his head. "I'll wait." Just as well, since Buff had already wolfed down the snack. He probably thought the green spots were healthy, like lettuce.

"Maybe we can grab a wink while he sleeps. We may not get many chances." Buff eased himself down to the floor and stretched out. Within minutes, he was snoring in a slow rumble.

Cable stretched out on the couch. It felt so good to close his eyes.

"Wake up, you lazy louts!"

Cable's eyes snapped open, and he glanced at his watch. Well, he'd gotten a couple of hours of rest, and he was going to need it in the times ahead.

Ketchum was reassembling and loading the Heckler & Koch, handling it like it was a baby.

"What's your plan now?" Cable asked, wondering if Ketchum missed Biff and Kale. He hadn't said a word about them, just stayed mad that they'd been taken.

"We're gonna watch and grab our opportunity."

Cable shrugged and put his Colt .45 automatic under his belt and reached for one of the AR-15s. Ketchum had the Colt Python in his belt, while Buff had a Smith & Wesson .38 in his and reached for an AR-15. Each slipped a couple of spare banana clips into their pockets. If they got the least bit of a chance, they were ready to turn the world into so much Swiss cheese.

"THIS IS NO WAY TO LIVE, always on our toes, and we're starting to run out of things. We could get by if it wasn't for the baby," Bonnie said. "I need milk, fresh veggies, and fruit for Little Al. Meat would be nice too. The freezer and cupboards are pretty bare. Old Mother Hubbard is all right as a story, but I hate to be living it."

"Al's down by the lake, isn't he?" Fergie asked.

"Yeah. Maury's watching the front side."

"Maybe I could make a quick dash, but don't tell Al. You know how he can fuss about things."

"Your things? If you call that fussing."

"You know what I meant."

"Perhaps, but Maury is starting to rub off on me." She went to look out from the upper back deck, where she could see down to the boat shed and fishing dock. "Yep. He's still there. I've already got a list of what I need."

Fergie got her keys and held Tanner inside as she slipped out the door. She looked around and couldn't see anything suspicious, so she got in her car and started up the drive.

Just a quick drive into town and back. What harm could that do?

KETCHUM WAS JUST BACKING the truck into a thick stand of sumac when he caught a glimpse of a car coming up to the end of Al Quinn's lane. He went backward faster so that they'd be out of sight when the driver got out onto the road.

As soon as he thought it was safe to pull out without being spotted, he drove onto the two-lane asphalt and took off at a pace that would let them keep the car in sight.

"You see," Ketchum said, "it's just like heaven to give us the opportunity we've been needing."

Cable thought heaven hardly had anything to do with it. Maybe the other place.

Ketchum held back as the car pulled into the big parking lot of an H-E-B Grocery. He was still slowly going up and down the rows when the redheaded lady got out and started across the lot toward the entrance.

"Damn, she's tall," Ketchum muttered.

Cable shook his head. "It's like that alien who landed and got out of his spaceship to meet an Amazon. He said, 'Take me to your ladder. I'll see your leader later.' I wonder how that Al Quinn fellow deals with that?"

"Go get the tape," Ketchum said. She had parked way out at the end of the parking lot, so he was able to park the truck next to her car.

Not in the mood for humor, Cable thought as he got out of the truck. He had been ready to add another tall-girl gag. "When you're nose to nose, your toes are in it. When you're toes to toes, your nose is in it."

Inside the store, he found the roll of silver duct tape he wanted in the household-goods aisle. Just about every other cart had a small child in it, and half of those were kicking up a fuss—crying or screaming for a toy or treat. He headed for the front of the store as quickly as he could and was checking out in the fifteen-items-or-less row and could see her filling up a cart. He took his purchase outside and headed back to the truck.

Chapter Eighteen

Fergie came out of the H-E-B Grocery pushing a cart full of fresh foods, meat, veggies, and milk—the things they were missing. She'd spent more than she'd planned to, but who knew how long they were going to be holed up with those jackals on the loose.

She had parked as far away from the front door as possible and near a rack where she could leave the cart. The distance gave her the illusion of getting in a hint of exercise and an opportunity to glance around to ensure no one was following her. She didn't think she had any reason to be suspicious, but she was always a little wary.

Just the usual sort of slow-driving people looking for parking spots nearer to the store's door roamed the rows as well as folks with loaded carts like her, hauling their grocery loot to their cars. She didn't spot anything out of the ordinary, although she was watching with a keener-than-usual eye.

As she got closer to her car, she saw a big red pickup had parked on the other side of the rack for carts. *What's the matter with people? Are they lonely? A great big parking lot like this, and they park near the vehicle that's all alone.* Then she thought perhaps an employee had parked way out there so the good spots closer in went to customers. She didn't see anyone in the truck, so she relaxed. As she got to the car, she glanced around again. Nothing.

Fergie unlocked her car and popped open the trunk. As she was putting the first bag in, thick arms wrapped around her and held her tight. Fergie snapped her head back, trying for a head butt, but whoever was behind her knew to watch for that and kept his head clear of hers.

Before she could scream, someone reached around and slapped a strip of tape across her mouth. She caught just a glimpse of the man with the tape before he put another strip across her eyes. Fergie thrashed and tried a backward head butt again, but whoever was gripping her so tightly that all the air felt pushed from her lungs knew enough to dodge her head.

She stomped down hard with a bootheel then kicked back as she was lifted off the ground. Whoever was behind her was big, at least as tall as her and with forearms like tree trunks.

The guy holding her grunted an "oof" but still held her tightly. Someone else grabbed her legs and wrapped what was probably more tape around her shins and ankles.

She struggled but could feel them wrapping her wrists together tightly. *Can't anyone in the parking lot see what's going on?* Maybe not, as far out as she'd parked.

They tossed her into a seat and fastened a seat belt around her. Then she heard the driver's voice for the first time. "Better get those groceries too. We can use the tucker."

She tossed her head about. Maybe someone would spot her bound in the backseat of the truck. Then she realized the windows were probably tinted, and they'd parked away from other vehicles. They made no effort to stop her from thrashing about.

Fergie twisted her legs and tugged at the tape binding her wrists behind her. But they had used a lot of tape. When they lifted her legs to tug off her boots, she tried to kick them. They anticipated that and kept clear. Then they tugged her cell phone from her pocket.

With the boots and phone went her last hope of being found and rescued. She struggled all the harder, but it was useless. One of them chuckled at her efforts, and that only made her madder and more desperate.

"Just one quick message, and we leave the phone," the one with the lower gruff voice said.

Fergie's mind raced. *Is that the man at the house who shot Tanner?* The more she thought about it, the more she realized it might well be him. It didn't make her feel any better about the pickle she was in.

They all got into the truck, the big one in the backseat with her. She tried to kick him, but he twisted her legs onto the floorboard and pushed her down there as well. Then the truck was moving.

When she realized she couldn't free herself, she calmed down and began to conserve her energy for when she got the least chance. She tried hard to be optimistic but felt tears of frustrated rage building up under the tape covering her eyes. Maybe there would be an opportunity later. They hadn't just killed her, so she must fit into their plans.

The truck hit every speed bump on the way out of the parking lot, and she could feel it turn on the smoother road and start picking up speed—nothing that would attract a cop but clipping along at a pretty brisk pace.

None of them spoke. She thought she heard the big one grumbling and mumbling, maybe rubbing where she'd stomped his foot. Fergie wished she'd done a whole lot more. A lot of her training had involved hand-to-hand combat, but those guys knew most of the same tricks and were seasoned veterans of scuffles. She had never stood a chance.

The truck finally pulled in at what she guessed was a convenience store. She could smell a hint of gas and heard the bell of a gas pump.

"Get a couple of burner phones. Use her money." The voice probably belonged to the driver, who she figured had to be Ketchum.

She tried a muffled yell or two, but when they didn't bother to try to stop her, she knew they were too far away for anyone to see or care about someone trussed up on the floorboard.

A door opened, and someone got back into the front passenger seat. "Nope. We'll have to swing over to Walmart."

That was the end of discussion for a spell. The guys were businesslike with what they were doing, all in a quite sinister way.

She listened to the sound of the road beneath them and tried to make out what direction they were going. But it was useless. She was turned around and befuddled after the first few miles.

Fergie wondered if she would ever see Al again—or Tanner, Bonnie, Maury, and Little Al. She doubted that very much. The men were killers and scummy low-life ones at that. The odds of her surviving were far less than zero.

AL HAD SPREAD LIFE vests across the deck of his bass boat, where he could crouch in relative comfort while holding the 30-06 and keep an eye on the lake approach to the house. Maury had the front lane for the shift. Theirs was a life reduced to military precision of wary watchfulness that left little room to savor all the many joys that made living worthwhile.

His phone buzzed that he had a message. The note was from Fergie, but as soon as he read it, he knew she hadn't written it.

We have your string bean and want a trade. Use your clout and spring Biff and Kale if you ever want to see her again.

Short and to the point but the most sinister message he'd ever gotten, since he knew who sent it. They were capable of anything, short of letting Fergie live.

His heart felt like it had slammed up into his throat as he leaped to his feet and got out of the boat. He clung to the rifle as he ran up to the house.

As soon as he was inside, Tanner got up and came rushing to him. Bonnie looked up from Little Al, who was asleep on her lap where she sat on the couch. She must have seen something in Al's face.

"What is it?"

"Where's Fergie?"

"She... She said we needed stuff, so she slipped off to the grocery. Why?"

"They have her. Those bastards have her!"

"*What?* What can we—?"

Al held up a hand and punched in Victor Kahlon's number as fast as he could.

Victor answered in a snappy tone. "Now what do you—?"

"They've got Fergie! No time to talk. I need a huge favor. I have no vehicle. Can you—?"

"I'm on my way."

VICTOR HAD BARELY PULLED up to the end of the lane when Al Quinn came charging out the front door. He ran and was halfway to the truck when Victor yelled out his window, "Leave the piece!"

Al slowed and tilted his head.

"Clayton's orders. If any shooting needs to be done, I'll take care of it and call for backup as needed."

Al frowned but took the gun out from the small of his back and ran back to the house. He opened the front door, and Maury took the pistol with one hand while holding back Tanner with the other.

Then Al sprinted back to the truck and slid into the passenger seat.

Victor started to pull away while Al was still closing his door. "Where to?"

"Head for the nearest H-E-B. I'll home in as we get closer."

Al took out his cell phone and stared down at the screen. Victor recognized the screen that was tracking a homing device.

"Is that for Fergie's cell phone?"

"Yeah, and another's for the transmitter in her boots."

"And?"

"Neither's moving."

"You said the message implied she's still alive," Victor said. "That they want to use her for a trade. Dare I ask for what?"

"For Biff and Kale. They were pretty open about who they are and what they want. Did you talk to Clayton?"

"You know I did, and you know what he said."

"He doesn't negotiate with kidnappers, unless he must, and I've never known him to go for a trade."

"This isn't the Cold War. You know he always brings that up."

"Don't I know." Al shook his head, stared down at the small screen. His expression flicked between fear and anger. "I'd sure feel better if these were moving."

"This electronic stuff." Victor nodded toward Al's phone. "That's part of what Huff and Meat were up to when they were at your place?"

"Yeah, it was supposed to keep track of us all. Help us in just this situation."

"They might have seen through that, especially after all the traps and snares in the woods. These are pretty savvy guys when it comes to this type of stuff."

Victor pulled into the H-E-B parking lot.

"Over there," Al said, pointing at Fergie's car, which was parked near the extreme outside of the other parked vehicles.

Victor pulled up beside Fergie's car. Al was out the passenger door before Victor could turn off the engine.

"I don't need to tell you not to touch anything."

"If you're going to process it, do so quickly. I need a vehicle."

"I'll have it taken to the department, gone over thoroughly, and delivered out to your place today."

"What am I supposed to do in the meantime?"

"Sit and wait for the next call. There'll surely be one."

Al leaned closer to the driver's-side window, pressing his face against the glass. "Her boots and phone are in there. The only means we had of tracking her."

"So there's nothing you can do just now except wait."

"Can you check the glove box?"

Victor shrugged. "I guess."

He went to his truck and came back tugging on a pair of latex gloves. None of the doors were locked. He easily opened the passenger door, flipped open the glove box, and looked inside. "Her piece is still in there. A Glock."

"Then everything happened really fast, and they didn't take time to search the vehicle. How about the trunk?"

Victor popped it. "Nothing here."

"So they took the groceries too. Damn bunch of hyenas."

"I'll get the car towed and take you home, Al. Let's hope they call and soon."

"And what do I tell them? That Clayton says no deal, go ahead and kill her?"

Victor picked up every sign that Al was boiling inside, as mad as he'd ever seen him. But there was nothing he could do—nothing any of them could do. And yes, there was a far-better-than-even chance they would never find Fergie alive. Getting her out alive was not where the smart money would be betting. Of course, he said none of that to Al.

"Just wait," Victor said. "Can you do that?"

"I can't say I have any choice."

"How do you feel?"

"Do you know that painting *The Scream*, by Edvard Munch?"

"Yeah."

Al gave a hollow sigh. "Now I know the depths of helpless, terrified angst that painting was seeking to convey."

Chapter Nineteen

When Victor dropped Al off at the front door of his house and the sheriff's department truck pulled quietly away, Al just stood there.

Maury and Bonnie were inside or posted around the property to protect it, but he wasn't ready to talk with them or anyone about Fergie yet.

The whole time Victor had been driving to the grocery, Al wanted to grab the wheel, commandeer the truck, and go as fast as they could. Not that any of that would have mattered. She was just as gone either way.

That was the worst, being able to do nothing and having no honest hope.

Tanner whined inside the door. The dog knew Al was home. But he stood and thought, recalling every moment he could of Fergie.

Al struggled to wrestle down the growing hot wad of anger, the really harsh urge to tear them apart with his hands. He had no vehicle, and even if he did, he had no place to go. The jerks would have to call him, and when they did, there was little he could do. Nothing, really.

Clayton would not let Biff and Kale out, even if it was to save a human life. Al had no say, no matter what Ketchum seemed to think.

The worst thing in the world was to start mourning someone who was still alive. All of it made him feel helpless, frustrated, and enraged. *Clayton wants those guys alive, but if they so much as harm a hair on Fergie's head...*

He made himself stop thinking that way. He had to stop. But he couldn't push it away, drink it gone, or exercise past the hollow urge to howl in pain.

Al pushed open the door and let Tanner come rushing to him with his white wrappings and eagerly wagging tail. Dropping to his knees, he hugged the dog, blinking hard to keep anything like tears of anger from getting out. He took what comfort he could from the soft fur he could pet and the licks he got.

While he held Tanner, he looked around the living and dining area, where he and Fergie had spent so much time recently. Everything was in the same place and looked exactly as it had before, except it felt empty, and he damn well knew why.

"He's back!" Bonnie called out.

Maury came thumping up the stairs from the basement with the baby in his papoose. In moments, he and Bonnie had joined in the group hug. They had all been through enough of this sort of thing before and knew the sort of thugs with whom they were dealing. Hope was a wispy little thing that barely fluttered at the edges of their clinging effort to reassure one another. Al held them close, but all he could think about was Fergie, and he sincerely doubted to the core of his being that he would ever see her alive again.

FERGIE'S HEAD WAS IN a whirl. She had fiercely fought them all the time they were trussing her with tape, and that had turned her around. Then she'd been tossed onto the footwell like a bag of potatoes. She guessed she was in the back seat because with her height, she sprawled from door to door. When they had gotten in and closed the doors, one of them jumped in with her and had to move her legs away roughly to make room for some pretty big feet.

The truck turned several times, and the pavement changed textures and sounds, but she had no idea where they were headed. The one stop they made was in a Walmart parking lot. She tried to make muffled screams past the tape across her mouth, but they must have been parked far enough away that they didn't think anyone would hear her mumbles. They did nothing to stop her, if she didn't count a casual kick to her stomach by the super-large feet.

When the passenger door opened again after they'd waited a spell, someone slid in.

"Got 'em?" Ketchum asked.

"Yep."

That was the end of conversation for the next several miles. The inside of the truck smelled of old oil, dust, and the scent of the men, whose bathing habits, or lack thereof, gave them the stale dried-sweat aroma of a condemned locker room.

She tried to formulate a metric for how many miles they had gone and in what direction. But she soon realized that was useless. The highway's grind and hum beneath them changed its textures, and the truck turned and turned again, to where she no longer had the least idea of where she was or where she might be going.

Fergie wondered how Al would respond to her sudden absence. Worse, he had to realize, as she did, how very slim her chances were of getting clear of the murderous oafs.

She tried not to think about any of that, but like any idea she attempted to suppress, the thoughts whirled around and around in her head like some maddening dream over which she had no control. Al would know she was probably going to die. It wasn't going to be fun for either of them. She had been a cop too long to think it could end any other way.

Fergie heard and felt the pavement shift to gravel as they turned into a drive. After a short while, the truck stopped, and the driver turned off the engine.

"Get her and the groceries inside."

Two of them lifted her and started to carry her. She snapped at the waist, bending back and forth to make it as difficult as possible. One of them slammed a fist into her thigh, not an idle poke either. The blow felt like an anvil falling on her. She stopped her twitching before she became a solid bruise.

They carried her inside. She guessed when they were at the doorway but knew when they plopped her sideways onto a couch. One of them started to walk away. The other one stayed near and poked one of her boobs with a finger.

"Leave her alone, Buff."

The finger poked again.

"I mean it. We need her okay for now. If things don't go well getting Biff and Kale back... Well, we'll see then."

She lay there, listening and trying to figure out what they were doing next. From the rustle of bags, they were bringing in the groceries.

"Got a lot of milk here but no beer. What kind of people are they?"

"We can always get some more beer. She had a fair bit of change in her wallet, though I don't think we dare use her charge cards. You're as tall as her, Buff, but I 'spect the name on the card would trip you up."

They put the groceries away, made themselves lunch, and left her alone. None of them spoke, but she could hear them eating. *What sort of people eat that loudly?*

That was okay for at first, although she couldn't speak or see. After a while, her body began to let her know she needed a trip to a bathroom.

"Mmfph. Mmfph," she managed past the tape.

"What is it, Miss String Bean Princess?"

She made the sound again.

"Can't hear you? Speak more clearly," the one with the deep, gruff voice said.

Finally, someone took the corner of the tape across her mouth and tugged it off.

"Bathroom," she said.

They had a discussion about that, one that went on long enough that the point nearly became moot. Finally, they stood her up, untaped her legs, and led her into a room that smelled badly of bathroom odors. They left her eyes covered and untaped her hands enough to tie the left one to something, perhaps the bottom of the sink. Then they left her alone in the room and closed the door.

She quickly took care of her business, got her clothing back in place, and considered whether she had any remote chance of escape. Not likely, tied as she was to the sink.

Fergie started to raise her free hand to her face to peel back the tape and have a peek around and perhaps see out a window and get some idea of where she was. But the door opened, and two of them came back in and led her back to the couch, where they rebound her feet.

Time seemed to pass in an unusually slow way, like pulled taffy or one of those Japanese Noh plays that went in slow motion. Whenever Ketchum had to make a call or answer one, he thumped across the floor with his cane and went slowly down the outside stairs. She wasn't privy to a single call, although she hoped Al and the men were in communication and was even more hopeful about her release. *But if I'm honest with myself...*

No. Stop. She wasn't going to be honest with herself. She had spent too many years on a police force to give herself even the tiniest ray of hope. So she wouldn't think about that at all, if she could. But she soon found she could think of nothing else—of the house, the others, and how much Al might miss her when she was gone.

She could smell gun oil. From the sounds, she could tell they were sitting around the table, cleaning their guns. No one had mentioned feeding her anything. They rarely spoke to one another and even then sometimes in grunts. Lying there helpless was like being in a cave with wild beasts. There was no television to watch, and she couldn't imagine any of them reading a book.

The evening dragged along with one more awkward bathroom visit. She managed one quick lift of the corner of her eye tape, enough to see that the sky was dark outside the small window, and she barely got the tape back in place in time. One of them handed her a plastic bottle of water long enough for her to take a quick drink before it was snatched away. Hell, the water had come from the groceries she had bought.

As they plopped her back onto the couch, one of them asked, "Should we feed her?"

"Maybe in the morning. We'll see."

"She's pretty skinny as it is."

"Probably not used to eating much anyhow." That sounded like Ketchum. "She'll last the night."

They made the usual sort of noises of settling in for the night—belching, farting, and occasionally coughing. Soon, it was silent in the trailer. The wind rasped against the metal roof, and after a while, a chorus of coyotes started in with their howling racket. Little voices of the pups joined in for a spell.

The floorboards creaked, and she heard a soft footstep, but it was a big foot. Someone reached down and put a hand on her chest.

"I said leave her alone!" Ketchum boomed.

"Aw."

"She's trading stock, so hands off... for now."

The last two words gave her a lot to think about as the place settled back into a creaky, raspy quiet. She didn't think she would ever fall asleep, that she couldn't or shouldn't. But in time, she did.

Chapter Twenty

Al was standing outside the front of his house, holding the 30-06 across his chest and watching the sky beginning to dim as the day faded into dusk, when Fergie's car followed by a sheriff's department cruiser came up the lane. He opened the front door and leaned the rifle against the wall.

Woodrow, an older deputy he knew, got out of Fergie's car as Al bent in to take a peek in the glove box to make sure Fergie's Glock was still there.

"All processed for prints and DNA," Woody said. "Didn't get none, but they had to try." He had a scruffy white mustache and was only a year or so away from retirement himself. "We're all hopin' you get 'er back, Al, but—"

"Yeah." Al knew the odds weren't good.

Woody waved as he climbed into the passenger seat of the cruiser, which backed around and headed back up the lane.

With a vehicle he could use, Al wanted to dash off and hunt for Fergie. But with nothing to go on, he had to wait. That was all he had been doing, and it had been hell.

He took a deep breath of the evening air and smelled cedar, dried leaves, and the musky hint of some woodsy creature moving about—probably a raccoon or possum, since the skunks and armadillos wouldn't be out until it got darker.

He turned and went inside, sat down at the dining table, and waved away an offer for a cup of coffee from Bonnie. Tanner came over to Al and pressed close to his feet. Somehow, he knew.

"I hate to bring up the subject, but we're back where we were about food," Bonnie said. "We're about out."

"How can you bring that up when Fergie's being held captive, and might not ever... Well, she was nabbed while getting groceries." Maury glanced at Al. "What's to keep these guys from watching our lane and grabbing whoever goes out next?"

"Bonnie's right, though." The fridge and pantry had been nearly bare when Fergie made her disastrous trip to the grocery, and that included milk for the baby. "We need provisions. That's the thing about terrorism, which this has become. When we're scared or unable to lead normal lives, then they are flat-out winning."

"But how?" Maury asked. "Will they try a grab again or come to the house while we're away?"

"I think we have to count on one thing," Al said. "It's Bonnie they're still mad at... and mainly because she wouldn't allow herself to be shot. These guys are driven, but they're far from logical. We just have to be careful about how we go about this."

"What do you have in mind?" Bonnie asked.

"First we have a scout around the property. Make sure no one is waiting to see us leave so they can follow. Then we all get armed and go together, baby, dog, and all, to the nearest convenience store. We get what we need as quickly as we can and scoot for home."

Maury said, "I wish..."

Bonnie was standing close enough that she was able to give Maury a quick jab in the ribs with her elbow to keep him from mentioning Fergie.

"Let's shake a leg," Al said. He slipped his SIG Sauer under his belt at the small of his back, petted Tanner, and headed for the front door.

Maury had Fergie's Glock and would stay with the baby and dog until Bonnie had returned from checking the lakeside.

Once out the door, Al took a deep breath, glad to be doing something, anything, even if it was an overly elaborate effort to get groceries.

That was what those men had reduced him and his household to, and they had Fergie. Clenching his teeth, he slipped into the woods and headed all the way up to the end of the lane. He wove through the trees, aware of every crunch, each step made, and he paused often to listen. A lot of little things were rustling through the leaf litter and twigs. He got near a bedded-down doe and went around her.

When he got all the way to the road, he stepped out onto it for a moment. Two coyotes gnawing at something saw him and turned tail to shoot into the trees on the far side. Next, he slipped back into the woods and went a mile and a half in each direction. He found the spot where he thought Ketchum had parked a truck to wait for someone to leave. They had probably wanted Bonnie, but Fergie was at least leverage to them.

Once satisfied no one was waiting by the road, he jogged back to the house. Bonnie was already loading the baby and Tanner into Fergie's car.

"You drive, Maury. Bonnie and I will go into the store, quickly get what we can, and be right back out. Keep your gun handy. This'll be a quick in-and-out mission."

They soon got to the nearest convenience store, a Circle K with an offering of the usual beer, sodas, chips, and jerky. But it also carried milk, bread, cottage cheese, and even some fresh fruits and vegetables.

Theirs was the only car in the lot. Al gave Tanner a pat as he got out. The store was about a half hour away from closing. They'd just squeaked in. Al glanced at the sign on the door that said carrying handguns inside was strictly against the law. He and Bonnie broke that law and went inside, their guns at least out of sight. She moved quickly to fill a handbasket while Al carried another one to hand to Bonnie when hers was full. They were nearly ready to check out when two men came into the store. One stayed by the door. The other went straight over to the clerk.

"Open the register, and empty it!" The voice was firm, as was the hand holding what looked like a revolver.

"Oh damn," Al said. He put a couple of cans of dog food into his basket and lowered it to the floor. Bonnie put hers down, too, and moved toward the door while Al headed for the cashier.

Al had his gun out and was six feet away when he said, "Drop the gun, and you won't get hurt."

The guy spun and saw that Bonnie stood by the door with her gun pointed toward him too. The unarmed, twitching accomplice yanked the door open and dashed outside.

But in seconds, he came back in with Maury behind him, holding him at gunpoint. "I told him he probably couldn't outrun a bullet," Maury said proudly.

The one with the gun lowered it to the floor and held up his hands.

"Call the sheriff's office," Al said. The clerk reached for his phone.

The two would-be robbers were young and scruffy. Both smelled of beer.

From the store's little hardware section, Al took a package of plastic cable ties and used them to handcuff the pair to each other. The younger one's blond hair had been cut into a Mohawk that had grown out enough to look a rat's nest. He was the nervous one, probably a first timer. The older partner favored some sort of slicking gel on his hair, if he ever washed it at all. He wore a brown hunting jacket while the blond one's jacket was a red-and-black check.

The front door opened, and as soon as Al saw the uniform, he put his gun away. Maury and Bonnie did the same.

As the deputies got closer, Al saw the belly of the sergeant and recognized them. They were Bob and Sandel, who had been out to Al's place to collect Kale and Biff.

They had both seen Al and the others hide their guns. Bob just laughed and reached for the robbers. The gun they had used still lay on the tile floor.

"Lucky for us you just happened to be here armed to the teeth," Sandel said.

"We were shopping," Bonnie said. "That Ketchum stole our groceries when he nabbed Fergie."

Bob's faced sobered. "I was sorry to hear about that, Al. Everyone at the department is pulling for you, but..."

"Yeah. With you, man." Sandel held out a hand, which Al shook.

"Tell you what," Bob said. "Since you did us a good turn, I can run it up the chain of command and see if we can't get a cruiser posted at your place long enough for you and yours to make a proper run into H-E-B while it's still open."

"I understand," the cashier said. "I can put the things you all picked out back on the shelves. Go into the H-E-B and get proper stuff. The sell-by date on our milk was borderline anyway. I appreciate what you done, and it's all up there on camera for the boss to see." He pointed toward a security camera over their heads.

Bob called for another cruiser to take away the robbers for booking and sent Sandel to Al's place while he escorted Al's carload to the grocery. Once there, he got out of his cruiser.

"You'd better leave your peashooter out in the car," Bob told Bonnie. He watched as she handed over her .38 Chiefs Special to Al. "They frown on guns in stores," he said and winked at Al.

The store still had a half hour before it closed, but Bonnie was soon headed back to the car with Bob in tow well before the deadline. Bob was grinning like a Boy Scout. She had bought him a small bag of the store's quite-tasty donuts in thanks for his doing a good deed.

"She was like one of those people on game shows who have a limited time to fill their cart," Bob said as they were loading the groceries into the trunk. "It was all I could do to keep up with her short legs."

"Tell me about it," Maury said.

Bob got back in his cruiser and escorted them home.

While Bonnie filled Bob and Sandel's thermos mugs with coffee, Bob leaned close to Al and said, "The okay to give you a hand came from all the way up—Clayton. Everyone knows about Fergie, and we're all pulling for you." He didn't have to say what all of them expected to happen, but Al knew.

As the two cruisers rolled away, each deputy waved an arm out their window.

Maury put Little Al to bed, Tanner curled up in a corner, and Bonnie hustled putting groceries away. At least they wouldn't starve. But the house seemed to grow quieter and emptier as Al stood there.

He tried very hard not to think, but his stupid brain whirled on and on.

Chapter Twenty-One

Later that night, Al lay awake, with one arm stretched out to Fergie's empty side of the bed. Tanner was snoring softly. The dog had gotten as close as he could to the head of the bed on the floor beside it and had plopped down to sleep there, guarding Al or at least wanting to be aware if he got up.

Al had always been brutally honest with himself. When he realized he was getting older, he'd retired. He'd expected to live out his days by the lake, fishing and rising each morning to be just a little bit older. Never in his wildest dreams had he expected to fall in love and be married. But by gum, he had. *Surprise, surprise.*

Fergie had sashayed back into his life years after being the worst prom date ever to cast him under her spell and rip him away from that solitary existence he had sought to embrace. When he realized he could care again, deeply, for another human being, he finally let go, and it had happened. The result was some of the most joyous days of his life.

At that moment, he faced the hardest brutality ever—the expectation that he would never see Fergie alive again. Given the sort of men with whom he dealt, he knew they fueled themselves on anger and lashed out at the world, him and his loved ones included.

Having drunk far too much coffee, he felt like a twitching bundle of nerves with heightened awareness, his thoughts whirling over and over. There was damned little he could do about getting Fergie back to see her or hold her one last time.

Tanner stirred, moaning, with his legs moving a bit. Perhaps he was dreaming.

Al threw aside his covers, half-mad at himself for being cozy. He got out of the bed on the other side to avoid stepping on Tanner, tugged on his clothes and boots, and went out to the kitchen to make yet another pot of coffee.

He must have been banging around more than he thought because Bonnie came up from the basement, wearing a red-and-black-checked robe that was Maury's. She blinked as she came into the light.

"Well, aren't you a bull in a china shop."

"Sorry. Did I wake you?"

"Me and all the sailors at sea." She came closer and shooed him away while she finished getting the pot of coffee going. "Kind of restless, eh?"

"Yeah."

"Have you any ideas?"

"One or two. As soon as I can, I plan to go in and have a powwow with Clayton."

"Do you think he'll bend?"

"I guess I'll have to wait and see." Al got up to look out the window to the lake, where fingers of light were just beginning to show on the horizon, making the edges of waves moving silver lines. "Wait and see."

AL SAT IN THE WAITING area of the sheriff's department, dressed for action and as tense as he'd ever been. He'd left Fergie's Glock in her car. He no longer had a badge or the right to carry a gun into the department. And if push came to shove, he was riled up enough to go at those kidnappers with his bare fists.

A deputy he knew, Sanders, finally came over to him. "He's here, and Victor's in with him. You can go in now too."

As soon as he entered Clayton's office, the sheriff rose and said, "I'm so sorry to hear this, Al. I wish—"

"Before you say, 'there was more I could do,' I want you to keep as open and flexible a mind as possible." Al stayed on his feet.

Victor stayed in his chair, looking up at Al. His face seemed to be cautioning Al to tread softly.

Al didn't care a whoop about treading softly. He would stomp with hobnailed boots if need be.

Before he could say anything, his phone rang.

He frowned but took it out of his pocket. "It's them." Al switched to speaker phone and answered, "Let me talk to her."

"I want to know if you've—"

"Let me talk to her." Al's voice grew sterner. *That has to be Ketchum.*

"Are you going to listen?"

"Let me talk to her!" Al shouted.

"Oh crap," Ketchum mumbled.

The sounds were probably those of Fergie being lifted to her feet and tape being ripped clear of her mouth.

"Al?"

"Right here. Are you okay?"

"I'm alive... and okay so far. My eyes are taped shut."

A muffled sound followed as they put the mouth tape back on.

"The deal is simple," Ketchum said. "Spring Biff and Kale, or you'll never see this scrawny gal alive again."

The line went dead.

Al slowly put the phone back in his pocket.

Victor and Clayton looked at each other.

"You know if we did that," Clayton rumbled, "their next request would be for you to turn over Bonnie, and you still wouldn't have Fergie back."

"How would you feel if these assholes had Bess trussed up and waiting to die?" Al asked. Bess and Clayton had recently celebrated their forty-seventh anniversary.

Clayton looked down at his desk then up again.

"Before you say there's nothing you can do, let me suggest something that just might fit within the parameters of your rigid policy about dealing with kidnappers. First, I'd be appreciative if you could call Meat Jenkins in here."

"You know that had to be a burner phone," Clayton said. "Something we can't trace no matter how we try."

"I know. I have something else in mind."

They waited in the office for the better part of five minutes before Meat Jenkins came bursting through the door, looking like he'd run all the way from his techie lab on the far side of the building. His pale face was flushed pink and had a patina of sweat. He had black hair and a thick beard and wore jeans, sneakers, and a rumpled white shirt that was stretched tight across his belly, which had made a home for many a pie, cake, or cookie.

"What's up?" He glanced first at Al then at Clayton and Victor.

"They found the transmitter you put in Fergie's boots, and they left behind her cell phone. They have her."

"We did all we could." Meat looked down toward the floor, though his belly was in the way. "I'm sorry."

"Kale's the able one of them right now, with just an injured hand," Al said. "He can move about. Could we get a transmitter on him, keeping in mind these guys know we might use them?"

"If it was me, I'd put one on him, expecting him to find it. But I'd get another on him or in him. Have him swallow it maybe. You'd have a day or so."

Al looked at Clayton and waited.

The sheriff seemed to pause an overly long time, weighing this and that, but he'd heard the call from Ketchum himself. Suddenly, the lines on his forehead went away, and at last, he spoke. "I see what you're saying. We wouldn't be letting him go or making a trade. We'd be using him to try to track Ketchum." He glanced at Victor. "Well, what the hell. This is Al, after all, and Fergie. I was at their damned wedding. Let's do it."

KETCHUM GLANCED OVER at the lump on the couch as soon as he'd hung up.

"Are they gonna spring Biff and Kale?" Buff asked.

"We'll see. We have the upper hand here. But we're gonna have to do something about that." He nodded at Fergie. "She's a righteous pain to feed and get to the bathroom. Cable, why don't you look around in the neighboring properties and see if you can't find a simpler way for us to keep a handle on her."

Cable nodded, felt to make sure he had his belt knife, and went out the front door of the trailer.

"Buff, you keep an eye on her while I stretch out. An eye, mind you, not a hand. You hear me? She's gotta sing sweet when she talks to that hubby of hers next. Get it?"

Buff frowned but headed over to the cooler while Ketchum went into the bedroom to stretch out. His damned leg wasn't getting any better. But he was thinking of sawing off the arm cast in a day or two to see if he was up to shooting with that hand. It had been a while, and he would like to know if he still had his skills.

THE TRAILER HAD BEEN quiet for a while. Fergie had lain awake though blind and unable to speak. Her nerves were screaming for her to get up and run. But she was trussed up far too well for that. She would have to lie where she was.

Hearing Al's voice and letting him know she was alive had been like getting a glimpse into a world she would never see or experience again.

Fergie heard, or thought she did, steps coming across the room. She could sense a big form kneeling next to the couch.

"Hey, lady." The man's hot breath hit her face and smelled of a combination of beer and unbrushed teeth. *Whew.*

"Think about it. Just you and me. Can you 'magine some of the things we'll do? I ain't been near a woman in a pretty long while, and I got me some catchin' up to do. How you feel 'bout that?"

How she felt was that her skin was crawling. In all her life, she'd never experienced anything creepier or slimier. And this was the guy wooing her, or so he thought.

Suddenly, the door opened. Cable must have returned. "Hey, whatcha doing?"

"Just havin' a look. You can too. Ketchum's havin' a nap."

"Naw. We're gonna have to rig her different if she'll keep for any kind of trade. Give me a hand with her."

"Okay."

Fergie far from enjoyed being talked about like some slab of meat sprawled across their couch. But for the moment, she could do damned little about it. *If I ever get the chance...*

"Hold her legs when I cut this."

One of them cut the tape around her legs. But the other, with large, firm hands, gripped her as if expecting her to leap up and run. *Fat chance.* It would have been into a wall, blinded as she was.

A chain rattled, and she felt it going around her left ankle, then came the click of a padlock being put in place.

The other end of the chain rattled off to somewhere. Then it was locked in place.

Before, she had entertained ideas of getting loose from the duct tape. All she had to do was get a start on one edge with her teeth or fingernails. *Now that's out the window.*

They left her wrists taped for the moment.

"Think that'll hold her?" Ketchum must have risen from his nap.

"Should unless she's got laser beam vision, which I doubt. How about these?"

"Might as well."

The tape across her mouth was ripped away then the one across her eyes. Fergie wondered for a second if she still had eyebrows. She blinked at the light, although the room was lit only by what came in through tattered venetian blinds. Blinking again, she looked at the three men. Letting her see them was far from a good sign. That meant she probably wasn't going to get the chance to identify them. They were sure nothing pretty to look at.

Ketchum squinted at her. He leaned on a cane and had a dirty formerly white cast on his right wrist, which she had seen Al break with the barrel of his gun after Ketchum shot at Tanner. His chin and cheeks were covered in a coarse dark stubble, while his face looked flushed. His clothes looked slept in, which made sense, since he had emerged from the one bedroom. Even the camo design of the shirt didn't hide how wrinkled it was. He looked grumpy and mad. She had expected nothing less.

The big one, Buff, she guessed, had a sly grin on his big mug, as if he'd shared some private time with her. Only in his head perhaps, but his intentions had been blatant enough. He was football-player huge, which explained the firm grip when he'd held her and the bruise she probably had on one thigh where he'd frogged her one with one of those ham-sized fists.

That left Cable, the sly-looking one. Dirty and proud of it. He wore a wrinkled brown khaki shirt with stains on the elbows and collar. He also had a belt knife in a well-worn sheath.

He held up the ring with two keys that went to her padlocks. Ketchum waved toward Buff, who took the keys eagerly.

A row of long guns leaned against the far wall, out of reach of the thick chain that held her. Pistols and boxes of ammo were piled on the table, also out of reach.

She was in a trailer and, from what she could see out one window, in some woods.

"I'm gonna be talking with your squeeze in a bit," Ketchum said. "I want you to talk real nice to him 'bout getting our pals back. You hear?"

Fergie had not said a word yet. She wanted to ask him why the changes, more freedom of movement for her, letting her see them, and all that. But she feared the answer she might get, one she suspected she already knew.

"I got this too." Cable held up an aluminum softball bat with a taped grip he'd leaned against the wall beside the guns. "It'll deter any surprise visitors, and it'll tame anyone who decides to get too frisky." He stared at Fergie. "It was lying around with that length of chain and just plain begged to come along."

Every word and gesture from the men so far had been to intimidate and bully her. She'd been on the police force too long to miss even the tiniest nuance.

"Do you think that now that you're better able to get around, you might be able to make us some dinner?" Ketchum asked.

"I could make you a salad." Her voice was raspy from nonuse.

"A salad! You hear that, boys? A salad." Ketchum forced a short laugh. "Naw. There's other stuff in those groceries. And why so damn much milk?"

"There's a baby. I got the milk for him."

"Hmm." Ketchum rubbed his raspy chin.

She probably shouldn't have told him that. He was the sort who might try to use that for more leverage.

"Well, move me to the kitchen, then. I'll see what I can do." It killed her to be nice to them, but she was buying time. And maybe she could find some rat poison or something in the kitchen. *Hope springs eternal.*

"Well, get cracking."

Cable undid the end of chain that had been looped around a steel pole near the end of the couch. He led and she followed as they moved to the kitchen, where he attached the chain end to the thick pipe beneath the sink. She could move about but barely.

While they grunted and grumbled around in the trailer, she searched the cabinets and was surprised to find a few pans, including a stock pot and some mostly chipped plates, bowls, and tarnished silverware. Fergie washed everything as best as she could and set about making a beef stew, one she'd planned for Al and the others. She hoped they'd picked up new groceries, especially milk for Little Al. What she'd bought looked like it was going to go to waste. The guys seemed the meat-and-potato sort.

She also made a cracker-and-cheese plate for them, mainly so she could eat some of that on the sly while cooking. As it turned out, she had been wise to do so, since they ate all of the stew and saved none for her. They ate like rabid pigs at a trough and left nothing behind. Then they unhooked her long enough that she could gather the plates and clean them in the sink before chaining her to the couch once more.

She tried hard not to judge them, to think their anger stemmed just from being in a different class from her. But they made that a stretch, priding themselves on animal cunning and ferocity, from the way they talked and acted. They enjoyed and savored anger.

Her hopes were that they would get a call from Al in some effort to set her free. Even if Ketchum made a deal, though, she was almost certain he would break his end about letting her go.

Chapter Twenty-Two

"You can really get people to swallow a transmitter as well as plant one on them?" Victor leaned closer to see the tiny devices on Meat Jenkins's lamp-brightened desk. Al stood on the other side, peering over Victor's shoulder to watch as well. A lot hung on Al's idea, and Victor was less sure of it the more he thought about it. *But what else can we do?*

"Yeah. It's done all the time. Let's say a doc wants to see how the inside of your gut is doing or some scientist wants to follow a snake or a bird."

"Where will the other one be?"

"In his boots. I'm betting he'll ditch those as soon as he can."

"It'd be nice if we had both to track him by." Victor thought they were so tiny.

"But these guys are far too clever and paranoid for that." Meat looked up at Victor. Some bits of doughnut were sprinkled across his black beard.

"Are they paranoid enough, do you think, to find a transmitter in a hamburger?" Al asked.

"I guess we'll see," Meat replied. "From what you said, this guy is the better-spoken and more-well-mannered of them. But they all probably eat like wolves, and we're taking him a bacon-and-cheese Whataburger with fries. We might as well have a timer outside his cell to see how little time it takes him to inhale that after all the bad jail food he's had to endure. Hell, I wish I'd ordered another one of those burgers for myself."

"Okay," Victor said. "Let's do this."

The three of them were waiting when the turnkey came out with Kale's plastic tray. "He ate everything but the wrapper," he said, "and he had it all down in under five minutes too. Wanted to know if he could have more. I kept my arms up high in case he went piranha on me."

They moved Kale out of his cell and walked him past Meat Jenkins, whose eyes were on the screen of his cell phone. As soon as he was past, Meat whispered, "It's in him."

"Make the call," Victor said to Al.

Al took out his phone and dialed Ketchum's burner phone. He answered on the third ring.

"I've pulled some strings," Al said, "and they're going to release Kale today."

"What about Biff?'

"He's still recovering and is bedridden, unable to move about yet. He needs a bit more recovery time."

"Well, you guys sure as hell whisked him out of the hospital fast enough."

"What about Fergie?"

"We'll see when Kale gets here."

"Let me talk to her."

She came on. "Al, I'm—"

The phone was grabbed from her. Al could barely hear her trying to finish the sentence as Ketchum hung up.

"DON'T YOU WANT HIM to know I'm alive?" Fergie asked as Ketchum shoved the phone back into his pocket with his good left hand.

"He knows."

"Will you set me free when your guy gets back to you?"

"We'll see."

"You're just going to keep me here cooking food that I paid for but don't even get to eat."

"I saw you sneak a piece of cheese like some little mouse in the wall. That's plenty-enough food for an Olive Oyl like you."

Fergie had been doing all the things she didn't do at home—the cooking, the dishes—all to keep some semblance of freedom, chained as she was, and stay alive. The worst was having to do such things for men like them. Buff ogled her constantly, while the other two mostly ignored her like some ailing pet that was going to have to be put down before too much longer.

When Al had called Ketchum, she'd felt a tiny tingle of hope. They were up to something. But try as she might, she feared the worst for herself. *These are not men of honor, nor are they clean or God's gift to women that Buff thinks he is.*

"Tell you what," Ketchum said. "What do you got in them groceries that could whip up a good welcome-home bite for Kale when he gets here?"

"There's plenty of salad stuff."

"There you go with that rabbit food again. Hell, we'd all end up skinny as you. Think stick-to-the-ribs."

"There's enough stuff to make a pasta dish, like spaghetti. Some of the tomatoes, onions, and mushrooms can go in the sauce."

"Yeah. Get crackin' with that."

She did, but while she went through the routine motions of cooking, her mind was a whir of pushing around ideas, thinking ahead to any possible opportunities. If she was to live through the end of the week, that might be all up to her, since Al was in an impossible place.

Could I use a pan of boiling water on them? Not likely unless it was one super-large pan, and they had firearms within easy reach. Fergie took in every object she could see and considered its potential as a weapon. Then there was the issue of getting clear of the damned chain around her ankle, which was chafing and starting to dig into her skin.

That was something she could get past, if she could just get free of the trailer.

She would have to think long and hard, but at least she had time for that while she lived.

Chapter Twenty-Three

Deputy jail guards led Kale out of his cell and took him to a room that looked like it was used for interrogations. His stuff was laid out on a steel table.

"Get into your clothes," the turnkey said. "They're turning you loose."

Kale couldn't believe it but started to yank off the black-and-white jail togs. He pulled on his own clothes, which hadn't been washed since he was caught hanging in the air. But when he got to his boots, he slowed and looked hard at the soles. They'd been removed and replaced. *So it's like that.* He grinned. That would be an easy-enough thing to fix.

The last thing they gave him was his wallet, and what money he'd had was still in it. He pondered for only a second or two that some of that had been Heck's, and the rest he'd picked up here and there. Kale always had an eye out for setting aside what scratch he could for a rainy day—or a sunny one.

One of the guards led him down the hall. He came out into a room with that detective, Victor something. And there was that Al Quinn fellow standing there as bold as brass.

"I'm going to get Ketchum on the line," Al said. "I want you to tell him we're setting you loose. Got it?"

Kale noticed Al had been careful not to say they were setting him *free*. He nodded.

"That you, Ketchum?" Al said after he'd made the connection. "Hang on. I got someone ready to talk with you."

Kale took the phone. "Hey, it's me."

"They seem up to anything? This is a straight-up trade?"

"I can't tell. I'll talk to you later 'bout that." He was damned if he would tip off those screws that he was onto them the least bit.

"You know to lose anyone following you, right?"

He glanced at Al as Ketchum spoke.

"I wasn't born yesterday."

"They shootin' straight 'bout Biff not being well enough yet to move?"

That was a tender point for Kale, since he'd been the one to shoot Biff. He knew Ketchum might still be more than a little tetchy about that.

"I don't know how Biff's doin'. They ain't let me see him. He's some-wheres else."

"No idea where?"

"Nope. Okay. I'll see you in a while."

"What're you gonna do 'bout wheels?"

"I'll manage. Always have."

"Well, make it happen. See ya."

When the line went dead, Kale handed the phone back to the Quinn fellow.

VICTOR LISTENED IN as Kale made a call to get an Uber ride into town. While Kale waited outside the chain-link fence for the car, Victor went over and got into the passenger seat of Nathan Hobart's small black Nissan. He was one of the youngest new deputies and thought it a hoot to get to use his own car to help track where Kale Durant led them.

The radio was on a country station, with some guy who seemed to think yodeling would come back into style. Victor reached to turn it off. He turned off the cranked-up AC, too, before he had icicles on his eyebrows. Nathan didn't complain, since his car was being commandeered.

"Yours is the kind of vehicle people hardly notice. We should be able to tail him without being spotted if you hang back enough," Victor told him. "You'll get reimbursed for gas."

"I'm just glad to be in on this. I didn't work here when that Al Quinn was a detective like you. But everyone who's talking about what's going on says he's a heads-up good guy."

"He did the same job for Clayton that I'm doing now. Some say he was the best detective ever. That gives me something to aim for and do as good or better. Plus, he's a friend."

When the Uber ride, a square monkey-shit-brown shoebox of a vehicle, showed up, Kale got in.

Nathan put his car in gear, and they were off. He stayed well back of the Uber car except when it made a turn. Then he hurried ahead so it couldn't get out of sight.

Victor raised an eyebrow when the car took them into Austin instead of out into a spot in the country. The temperature was warming up into the eighties by the time the car pulled into a Walmart parking lot.

Kale took a minute or two to pay and got out then waved as the Uber driver went away.

"Park, and keep an eye on him. Move closer when you can without attracting his attention."

Kale moved about among the parked cars, peering into them and slipping quickly from row to row. Finally, he seemed to find what he was looking for. Someone had left their windows cracked and the AC running for a small dog inside a white Toyota Corolla.

Kale reached through the window and popped the door open. He picked up the yipping small white ball of fur and put the dog in the backseat. Before he got in, Kale tugged off his boots and twisted off the heels. He threw those out onto the parking lot's asphalt.

"There goes one tracker." Victor was leaning out his window, getting the whole thing on video with his cell phone.

As the Corolla pulled out of the lot, Nathan fell in behind it.

"That fella must have balls of brass," Nathan said. "Just out and committing grand theft auto—a felony."

"He doesn't know we're back here taping an account of his life in crime." Victor sent a copy of the video to Clayton. "We can add dognapping to his charges too. This guy does live large."

Traffic became heavy as they made their way out of the city and onto a main highway. They hung back and let the Corolla have some space.

The right lane was slowed by a dump truck and a cement truck crawling along below the speed limit, slowing even more as they climbed a hill. Cars shot around as soon as they could squeeze into the flow in the faster lane.

When they finally got around that tangle and started moving at a regular speed again, Victor looked ahead frantically. "Where is he?"

"I don't know. I could see him one minute but not the next."

Victor checked his phone, looking for the blip of the tracker inside Kale. "Take the next exit. We've got to go back on the access road."

Nathan went down the next ramp, made a left at the first turnaround he came to, and headed back in the other direction. After a mile or two Victor said, "Grab the next turnaround you see."

Nathan did and headed up that access road.

"Slow down." Victor pointed ahead. Kale was at a gas pump at an Exxon station. "Helluva thing, him having to buy his own gas."

"A shame," Nathan agreed. As they pulled up beside the station, they could hear the small dog yipping. "You'd think the owner of a car you steal would have the courtesy to furnish a full tank."

When Kale got back in the car and pulled away from the gas station, they followed.

"How are *we* on gas?" Victor asked.

Nathan glanced at the dash. "In good shape. This thing will go across Texas on a thimbleful."

"Well, bless Meat Jenkins for his transmitter, or we would have lost Kale in the shuffle."

Victor kept thinking the car would turn off onto more of a back road soon. No such luck, Victor realized, as they followed it onto a highway heading west. The car kept right on rolling toward the horizon.

Instead of stopping or giving any sign of heading for Ketchum's hideout, Kale crossed the county line, rolled on through that county, and was entering the next when Victor called Clayton.

"He's heading west like the dickens," Victor said. "I think he's taking it on the lam."

"Reel him in before he gets to New Mexico," Clayton told him.

Easier said than done. They couldn't PIT the guy or turn on flashing lights.

Victor was considering his possibilities when Kale eventually made his decision for him. He took an exit ramp, went along the access road, and turned into a Whataburger stand. That last meal at the jail must have been weighing on his mind.

He left the windows cracked, with the yipping small dog in the back, and went inside.

Victor and Nathan watched him make an order and go sit at a table, placing the number they'd given him so the server could find him.

Once the server brought his food then turned to head back to the counter, Kale reached for the paper-wrapped burger with his good hand. Victor brought a handcuff down on that wrist, stood Kale up, and twisted his other hand back to cuff them behind him.

Kale glared at them, taking in Nathan's uniform. "Hey, you don't have no jurisprudence or anything."

"You mean jurisdiction, and the honeymoon's over. Where the hell were you going?"

"I wasn't going nowhere where Ketchum could get his hands on me. Biff was his best bud, and he doesn't appreciate that me shootin' him was an accident, plain and simple. I figured it'd be best if I headed for somewheres else."

"Where is Ketchum?"

"Damned if I'll tell you that. He'd kill me twice if I told."

Victor picked up the burger Kale had ordered and handed it to Nathan. "We'll caravan back together. I'll drive the Corolla once we've secured this flight risk in it."

"Least let me have a bite to eat."

"It's back to prison food for you."

They used another set of handcuffs to fasten one of Kale's legs to the bottom of the Toyota's back seat. He wasn't going anywhere. Victor moved the dog to the front seat, which it seemed to prefer as he got out onto the road with Nathan trailing behind him, taking big bites out of the burger as he drove.

"You took my hamburger. That makes you thieves."

Victor didn't bring up that the cash Kale carried had probably come from Heck or another of the bunch's victims.

"You going to tell me where Ketchum is?"

"No."

"I hope they feed you nothing but wallpaper paste when you're back in jail."

Victor called Clayton once they were rolling as they headed back to the east. "Got him. I've got the stolen car, too, and a little white dog." The dog had curled up on the passenger seat on a warm spot created by sunlight coming in through the windshield. He had a silver paw-shaped tag that hung from his collar that read Alfie.

"The owner called about the car, but she was more worried about the dog. I'm glad you have them both."

"The one thing we don't have is Ketchum's location."

"That's not going to please Al or me either, for that matter."

"We'll just have to keep trying."

"The odds aren't getting any better with each tick of the clock," Clayton said.

Chapter Twenty-Four

Al's phone rang.

"Where the hell is Kale?" Ketchum asked. "You said he was being let loose."

"He was, and I arranged it. But your guy buggered off. Headed west like a bolt of lightning. He said he was afraid of you, that you would kill him for accidentally shooting Biff."

"That's a whale of a story. How do you know what he said?"

"Because he stole a car, like the idiot he is, and is now back in the slammer for auto theft. He stole a little dog too."

"What the hell would he want with a little dog?"

"I suspect it came with the car."

"Right now, the deal doesn't look very good. The skinny redhead may not make it through the day."

"She's not the one you want anyway. I can't help it if your own men aren't loyal to you. But if you want to settle this right, why don't you prance your stupid redneck ass over here in your sissy shoes and take care of business properly."

"Are you...?"

"That's right. I'm calling you a coward and a lily-livered one at that. The sheriff's men aren't watching my place right now. Come after what you want. But I won't be expecting you. You don't have the sand for it. All you can do is talk and whine."

The line went dead, and Al looked up to see Maury and Bonnie staring at him, their eyes wide. Bonnie was holding Little Al, who was asleep with his face pressed against her shoulder.

"What the hell did you just do?" Maury asked.

"The only thing I could do to agitate this madman to come at us. It's the only chance I have to free Fergie, and if it's too late for that…"

"Oh, Al," Bonnie said, "don't even think that."

"I have to, Bonnie. The chances are far better than even that Fergie won't make it through this." His voice caught a little. Al paused for a second. "So I'm doing the only thing I can do. Get this guy fired up to come here. This guy has buttons, anger ones, and I'm pushing them as hard as I can to get him coming this way."

"You're even thinking of turning Bonnie over to him?"

"No. She won't be here. Just you and me, Maury."

"I want to stay if there's gonna be a scrap," Bonnie said.

"Bonnie, you are hands down the best shot of us. But you've got to be clear of here. You're going to take a couple of guns onto the boat with you and get Little Al away from here. You'll stay away until we call you. You hear? Until it's all clear."

"I want to—"

"It's for the best, Bonnie," Maury said. "You have your priorities for protection. Al and I will do what we have to do." As he said it, the color washed out of his face, though he tried to stay brave and upbeat. "This guy's a madman and has proven it by time and time again trying to come after you. So you're the bait this time, but you'll be out of reach, where he can never get to you. Please. Do this for all of us."

"Well." Bonnie let out a huff of air. She turned and went down the stairs with Little Al to get ready for what promised to be some trying times.

"It was the only card I had left to play, Maury," Al said.

"I know." He shook his head. "I know."

The whole time Fergie had been held, and Al had no idea where, he'd been feeling helpless. If there was to be any hope, he had to wave the red flag in front of Ketchum and depend on the man's characteristic short fuse. Maybe it was too late for Fergie. Maybe not. He didn't want to think about that, yet he couldn't stop himself.

He mumbled, "I can't believe I said 'lily-livered.' My gosh, I'm a goof when I'm desperate." But his thoughts were still fixed on Fergie, and he doubted he could do anything to change that.

CABLE HAD A GOOD IDEA of how the call had gone from the way Ketchum shoved his phone back into his pocket. "Okay. Okay. Okay. This guy wants war, he's gonna get war."

"Do we kill the girl?" Cable asked.

"She's hardly a girl. This Al Quinn and his Fergie are both in their sixties. Retired, don't you know. Besides, we might need her for leverage before this is over. Biff's still in lockup. But for now, this guy's practically throwing down the red carpet and daring us to come."

"Doesn't that sound suspicious to you?"

"Screw suspicious. This is my chance at that bitch that shot me. I owe her big time. I'm gonna collect. Get the string bean cooking up something, and let's see to our arms. We lost a fair bit of guns and ammo in the lake."

"We still have a couple of AR-15s and enough handguns and ammo." Cable got his Colt .45 out of his backpack and slid it under his belt—it felt good to have it there, like a good friend. He had a hunch he would be glad to have a good friend along.

"Sure wish we had those grenades and maybe a grenade launcher. What we do have is an element of surprise."

"How can this be a surprise? He knows you're coming," Cable said. "Seems like he practically invited you."

"I don't think he believes it yet, but he will soon. He'll know it like a bullet," Ketchum said. "Buff, you're gonna have to stay with the redhead. We may need her yet. When the time comes we don't need her, well..."

"If you say so." Buff's eyes lit up with a sinister glint.

"Just don't damage the merchandise. She needs to be breathing and more or less healthy."

FERGIE HAD MIXED FEELINGS as she made sandwiches from a loaf of Jewish rye that had been among the groceries she'd bought for her household. She made the usual ham and Swiss with spicy mustard along with bologna sandwiches with ketchup. Maury was the one at their house fond of bologna, and Bonnie had grown up with it too. She should be making the sandwiches for them instead of these kidnapping jerks.

For a while, Fergie thought she was fighting a losing battle to prepare food for them. As soon as she made one of the bologna sandwiches, Buff grabbed it off the plate and wolfed it down. He finally slowed after six sandwiches, and she put the rest out for Cable and Ketchum. She'd seen Ketchum watching her, daring her to steal a scrap of *their* food, which was laughable, since it was food she'd paid for, but their sense of ownership went to anything they had stolen as well as earned.

Ketchum and Cable debated about whether to go across the lakefront properties or drive the truck closer and move in from there. Finally, they decided to use the truck, so they started loading guns and ammo into it. Just as the evening was settling into dusk as the sky darkened, they climbed into the truck and, with a small spray of mud and gravel, were gone.

Well, that narrows the odds, Fergie thought. But Buff probably counted as more than one person guarding her. Maybe she could outrun him, if she could get shed of the damned chain.

She was still cleaning up the dishes when the truck came back to the trailer. Ketchum and Cable came inside.

Cable took the end of the chain going to Fergie's left ankle and took it into the bathroom and fastened the other end to the plumbing under the sink. That had been an afterthought and one that dimmed her chances at any kind of foot race, even if she'd been able to get the damned chain off.

"What if I have to use the bathroom?" Buff asked.

"Go outside, or work around her. She's not gonna see anything new to her."

"But maybe not the same size." Buff gave as sinister a grin as Fergie had ever seen.

Ketchum shook his head.

Cable brought over the silver aluminum softball bat with a taped handle that said it was a Worth bat called a Thumper. "If she gives you any fuss, you can calm her down some, but don't kill her... yet." He went out of sight.

"C'mon," Ketchum said.

Then she heard the door slam, and she was alone with that stupid sex-starved Buff.

The nerves of her skin rippled. Nothing about her current situation encouraged her or made her feel good... or at all safe.

Chapter Twenty-Five

When the truck pulled away, Fergie was alone with Buff, with her chained in the bathroom. The thought of having to sleep on the filthy bathroom floor worried Fergie, but Buff gave her far, far more reason for concern. He'd been sniffing about her since she'd been hauled out to the godforsaken place. He had to view the moment as his chance.

She went across the room, about as far as her chain would let her go, and turned the flimsy lock on the closed door. It didn't look like it would do much good if someone was determined, especially someone as big as he was.

Fergie could hear his giant feet plodding around in the trailer, sometimes coming to the closed bathroom door then going away.

She went over and tried to open the small window, though she wasn't even sure she could get through it if it opened. But it was jammed tightly shut and was too high as well. Then there was the damned chain to think about. A coyote might gnaw off a leg to get out of a steel trap, but she'd probably just bleed to death.

Fergie was as sure as she was breathing that the day was her last one on earth—she would die before dawn.

She had heard enough of Ketchum's side of the conversation with Al to guess that the suggested trade had not gone well. Maybe that had somehow kept her alive. She had figured Ketchum would kill her as soon as he had his chums come back. He still needed her for the future. But as soon as he got his way, she would be of as little value as a used tissue, and he would kill her as brutally as possible. Her brain raced as she considered possible ways she might get free, but her flurry of thoughts was getting nowhere, and that only added to her frustration and fear. She hated to admit that those guys had her genuinely afraid, because that would only make them happy.

Time was stretching out. She waited and waited, hearing him out there clomping about, probably to the beer cooler often. It might be hard for him to be patient with the others gone, leaving him behind. Or he could be working up a righteous buzz to do something crazy. He was already dangerous. Drunk and dangerous could hardly be an improvement.

She wondered how Al, Maury, and Bonnie were faring with the arrival of Ketchum and Cable. Al and the others couldn't be in much better shape than she was.

After what seemed a lifetime, the heavy footsteps came to the bathroom door and stopped.

"Hey, pretty lady. You wanna come out and play?"

That was the way he made sweet talk, and it was as chilling and sinister as she could imagine.

She wanted to shout, "No!" To tell him to go away.

"Hey, c'mon, now. Open up. You don't want to make me angry. I'm not so pretty and kind when I'm riled up."

Oh lordy. To those guys, anger was a religion. She didn't answer but stared at the door. It didn't look all that sturdy. But if he broke it in, the others might give him a hard time about that. There wouldn't be privacy in there anymore. But with that lot of barbaric men, maybe that didn't even matter.

Thump! Something banged hard against the door. If she had to guess, she would put money on it being the metal bat.

Thump! There it was again. Then he began to hammer at the door in earnest.

She had been right. The door was far from sturdy. It began to bend and splinter in. Fergie could see him outside, banging away at the door with that silver aluminum softball bat. His face was flushed a bright red.

His eyes were squinted yet throwing sparks of fury. Well, she had indeed managed to make him mad.

She stood up straight, waiting for him to burst through the remaining fragments of the door.

Buff got through at last and came rushing toward her like some enraged, red-eyed bull.

Fergie was poised and ready. As soon as he was near her, one arm outstretched to grab her, she let go with a field goal kick with her free leg that would have put a football through the uprights from fifty yards away.

"Oof." His eyes crossed, and he grabbed his crotch, letting go of the bat, which dropped to the floor with a clatter and rolled toward Fergie.

She scooped it up and, without a hesitating a second, swung it to clang against the side of Buff's thick skull. It made such a pleasant sound to her that she did it again.

He dropped to his knees, his eyes rolling up in his head. He might have already been out for the count, but she swung again from the other side. The bat made a joyous peal that would have been recognizable to those long-ago fans of *The Gong Show*.

Buff fell face down on the floor. She had to do a lively hop to keep his giant head from landing on her chained foot. His head made a thump that nearly shook the trailer off its cement blocks. She leaned closer. Yep, he was out for the count and then some.

Cautiously, she moved closer, in case he might be faking so that he could grab her. But it was like Bonnie said: "When a possum starts to swell, you know it ain't fakin.'"

Buff was indeed not faking. His face was pressed against the floor, and he didn't look like he would stir for a long while. Fergie dug into his right jeans pocket with a couple of fingers and came out with the two keys that went to the padlocks.

She undid the lock on the chain on her leg and removed it, rubbing at the chafed red lines around her ankle. *Bunch of barbarians!*

To get to the lock holding the chain to the bathroom's sink pipe, she had to bend low and look up. As soon as she had it unlocked, she took that freed end of the chain and headed over to Buff. His arms were at his sides, so she was able to lift one wrist and wrap one end of the chain tightly around it. She lifted the other arm, which felt as heavy as a side of beef, wrapped it with the chain as well, then padlocked the wrists together.

She had a long length of chain left, so she lifted one ankle, drew it close, and wrapped it in the chain. Then she brought the other end up to the other ankle, wrapped it as well, and padlocked his ankles together too. As strong as he was, she doubted he would get the best of that chain.

Out in the living area, she went to the cooler and took out a bottle of water. She was hungry but left the food alone. It had been pawed over. Buff had pulled the remaining slices of bologna out of the wrapper and wolfed them down at some point. What she really wanted was to get the hell out of there.

But she spotted the roll of duct tape on the breakfast nook table. "Oh, what the hell." She picked it up and went back into the bathroom then tore off a strip and stretched it across his closed eyes and put another bit across his mouth. "We'll see how you like being treated this way."

When she stood up, she resisted the urge to spit on him. Al had said that no matter how animal-like the men were with their anger issues, it was up to Al and her to rise above that. Dammit, he was right.

Fergie glanced around. All the remaining weapons they'd had were gone. She went back to the bathroom once again and picked up the silver softball Worth bat, which read Thumper on its side. The bat had lived up to its name and had done a thumping good job on Buff.

Her boots were long gone, so she was in her stocking feet. Nothing in the trailer looked like it would serve as shoes, so she would have to go as she was.

Fergie went to the front door and stepped out into the cooling air as dark settled in. She had no idea of where she was, but like the walk of a thousand miles, she took the first step and headed up the lane.

Chapter Twenty-Six

Cable glanced over and saw the look on Ketchum's face. He'd seen that expression before—like flames straight out of the fireplace in a rage. "Ain't we gonna park somewhere kind of close and sneak in?"

He glanced at the speedometer. They were going almost seventy on the two-lane winding back road and slid on the gravel of the shoulder a time or two on tight turns. Ketchum just gripped the steering wheel tighter.

"I think we'll surprise them with a little something different this time." Ketchum's teeth were nearly clenched. "That bitch's time has come."

Cable had expected that sooner or later Ketchum might just go borderline suicidal. At that moment, Ketchum's eyes were in a fixed stare, and a bit of drool was coming from the corner of his mouth.

"I could sneak in and turn off their electricity," Cable suggested.

"What would that do?" Ketchum gave him a quick glance.

"Disrupt them. Get them off balance."

"They'll be plenty off balance when we open fire."

"I could cut their phone line."

"They'll have cell phones."

"I was just thinking we could be more cautious in going about this."

"Are you with me or not?"

"I'm with you." Cable thought back to those days he'd heard about in Vietnam, where many a gung ho second lieutenant got his Purple Heart the hard way by being shot in the back of the head by some reluctant PFC. Yet he also knew he was somehow bonded to Ketchum through the years and would do what he wanted, no matter how crazy it was. Life was complex when he thought about it, which was why he rarely thought about it. He just lived it as it came along.

"I'm not planning a Pickett's Charge here. I just want you to keep them busy at the front of the house while I sneak around the back way."

"That sounds okay. Are you moving around better?"

"I'll be all right. Won't be long before I'll be tossing the cane aside."

Cable wouldn't have been surprised if Ketchum drove at the current speed right up to Quinn's door, slid sideways in the gravel, and hopped out to start shooting away. But with one leg still not perfect, that scenario seemed less likely, which was probably just as well.

When they neared the road end of Al's lane, Ketchum drove past it to where they'd stashed the truck before. Thick clumps of trees and bushes hid it from even the most careful eye of anyone driving by on the road. Although it was dark, Cable cut down a couple of sumac plants into five-foot lengths and went back to sweep away the tracks the truck's tires had made.

Back at the truck, he took one of the AR-15s, shoved four extra thirty-round banana clips into his pockets, and slid his Colt .45 automatic under his belt at his belly. Ketchum had an AR-15 and the Colt Python under his belt as well as the Smith & Wesson .38 revolver. He meant business.

They started off in single file through the woods, with Cable leading the way and at a slow pace so that Ketchum could easily keep up in spite of having to use a cane on ground that sometimes had soft spots.

Ketchum started, "Can we—"

"Go faster? No. Unless you want to wind up dangling like a Christmas ornament the way Kale did. Hmm?"

"Just go."

Cable continued to pick his way with extreme care, even though he could hear Ketchum grumbling. What puzzled him so far was that he found where some of the snares and pits had been, but the snares had been removed and the pits filled in. *Did this Al fellow just move them around to fool any trespassers?* He slowed and looked more carefully, though he could hear Ketchum fuming behind him.

As intensely as he looked, he could only find signs of traps and pitfalls being removed. None of that made him feel more confident. He moved even more slowly and paused only once or twice to shush Ketchum, whose grumbling was getting louder.

What bothered Cable most was why they would remove their defenses. It made him think they had lined up something different and far worse. It was what he would have done.

He stopped and listened intently. Ketchum bumped into him but only stopped and grumbled.

The wind moved the upper limbs of the trees some, and leaves were rustling about. But he heard no lizards, skunks, armadillos, or any other stirring night creature. The woods seemed preternaturally still. He didn't like that a bit.

"Come on. Can we pick up the pace a little here?"

"You want to take the lead?" he asked Ketchum.

"No."

"Then don't push me to move unwisely."

That shut him up for the next quarter mile or so of Cable moving as silently as the wing of an owl, with Ketchum crunching along behind, kicking leaves and occasionally breaking twigs.

Once they were closer to the house, Ketchum stopped Cable. "You wait here. Give me ten to fifteen minutes to get around to the other side, where I hope to get a shot at that bitch. Soon as that's in the bag, our work here is done."

He took off and was soon limping into the darkness and into such a tangle of vegetation that Cable could no longer see him, although he heard the crack of a limb breaking against the ground. He was relieved to be alone at last and continued to look carefully around. The idea that the Quinn bunch had taken down all their defenses seemed preposterous. That they might fear hurting deer and other woodland creatures seemed absurd, although they might well be just the touchy-feely sort to do something like that.

Cable was glad Ketchum had assigned himself the task of going after that Bonnie woman. He wasn't even sure what she looked like, except Ketchum had described her as a round little thing who shot far better than women were ever supposed to. Cable had only seen her from afar and barely the top of her curly blond hair as she was shooting a hole in their boat big enough to eventually sink it. He was also glad Ketchum was heading for where he could get some gratification or revenge. Once that was out of his system, maybe he would act less like he was headed for the bug house. Cable had known him a long time but had rarely seen him quite so twitchy and strung out.

Moving silently from tree to tree, Cable used the little light that filtered through the treetops to pick his way. Most of the bushes, he could brush aside, but he couldn't see enough of the leaves to avoid an occasional mesquite tree and its defense system of thorns. He twitched at each stab but stayed quiet as he worked his way up through the woods until he could see the house. Lights were on inside, so they were home. He sighted in on the house and could clearly see the front door, then he hunkered down on his haunches to wait, giving Ketchum the time he wanted to get to the back of the place.

He held the AR-15 across his lap and stroked its side. The woods settled into the usual creaks of limbs rubbing together, small scaly creatures skittering through the leaf litter, and the nearly silent soft-feathered swoop of an owl as it swept between the trees and landed talons first on a mouse that gave a sharp squeak before it died.

FERGIE FELT LIKE SHE had been walking along the lane for quite a long time, ages, although that could have been because she was in her stocking feet and was stepping on gravel more than half the time. She tried to place her steps in the hard-packed mud of ruts, but the Texas caliche soil, with its embedded pebbles and sharp rocks, had set like concrete and stabbed her just as heartily as the gravel had.

When she finally realized she had gotten to the road, she let out a big sigh. Then she looked around and saw that she was only about two miles down the road from home.

Her feet were sore, and she was tired. But she took a deep breath and started to run up the road toward their house. She could hardly wait to see how relieved they would be to see her, to know she was alive. For a moment or two, she wondered if Buff had awakened and how he might feel about being treated the same way they had her. She would have chuckled if that didn't mean spending breath she needed to keep running. The asphalt was flatter than the lane had been, but her already-sore feet were complaining. She ignored them and kept them moving.

Fergie ran on the left side of the two-lane road to face any oncoming traffic and step aside to let them pass. There was always the chance that some good Samaritan would pause and offer her a ride, but no such luck. Three pickups and a car with an overly loud muffler all thundered past like they were in the Indy 500. That was okay. She was getting closer to home with each step. Fergie went past a red-tailed hawk sitting on a fence post, on the hunt. It took to wing as she got closer.

She jogged regularly, so the run itself wasn't a trial. But she sure wished she had on her running sneakers. Even wearing her boots would have been better than chugging along in her socks. In a long pause between vehicles on the road, she glanced up at the stars, grateful to be able to see them and appreciating life so much more after her ordeal. But she wasn't prepared to thank any of those men. She would just as soon give them the treatment she'd given Buff. Thinking of that caused her to glance down, and she realized she had come away with the softball bat and was carrying it like a baton in a relay track and field event. That might be one reason no one had stopped to offer a ride. She nearly tossed it into the woods she ran past but thought, *What the hell?* She'd carried it that far, and it was doing no harm. So she ran on along the black stretch of road.

Chapter Twenty-Seven

Ketchum didn't have Cable's night eyes. His wide-swinging route around the house took him far longer than he had expected.

His first few steps were quick as he hurried. Then he froze, picturing Kale swinging in the sky after being snared. So he slowed way down, taking every step with care. By staying in the darkest part of the woods surrounding the house, he'd made a real chore for himself against a rough deadline. His fault, though he'd be damned if he would admit to it.

He'd told Cable to start shooting away in fifteen or twenty minutes, so he began to hurry, which was always a mistake in the dark. Since he hadn't thought to bring along a flashlight, he was making his way with what little light came from the sky. Not wanting to get too close to any of the house's windows, he wove through the trees and bushes a good twenty yards away. What little light came from the sky and the glow from the house didn't do much to help him. He bumped into trees and bushes, many with stickers. He could make out the shape and look of prickly pear cactus and was careful to skirt around it.

He could sometimes see through the trees enough to look down the three levels that led to the lake. He saw the fishing dock then the boat shed, which was empty. They'd fired out at the lake from there before. He wondered where the boat was.

Any pondering on that halted the second he heard shots coming from the front of the house. Cable had, as directed, opened fire and declared war on the house. Their attack had begun, and he was out in Bumfart, Nowhere, in the woods.

As soon as the shooting started at the front of the house, something moved below. Al Quinn popped out of where he had been hiding in some bushes next to the boat shed and ran up the stairs to the house, glancing to his left and right.

Ketchum darted as fast as he could to get behind a tree to keep from being seen.

Suddenly, he felt nothing but air beneath his cane and one foot. He'd been right on the edge of a small cliff.

As he fell sideways, he tried to remember how far down it was to the next level—ten or twelve feet at least. He hit with a thud and began a thumping roll into a big agarita bush, which was prickly with its hard and sharp holly-like leaves. He couldn't see the plant, but he didn't have to in order to know what was stabbing him all over. He rolled off it onto hard flagstones that ran beside the cement steps that led from the house down to the docks.

He stopped himself just in time before he rolled any farther and went over the next small cliff, where he would have fallen down to the lake level.

His arm hurt from where he had tried to break his fall, and his wounded leg was screaming at him. He doubted he had torn any stitches, but something inside the leg was burning with a real protesting flame of fire.

Some animal or bird in a tree above him made a sound that seemed to be mocking him, a hearty laugh at his expense. Then that faded away, and he could hear only the wind in the treetops.

After he had caught his breath, he lay there for a minute and a half while shooting and return gunfire went on above him. Cable must have been wondering what happened to Ketchum. He could hardly have guessed that he lay sprawled across gravel and grass halfway down to the lake and the water's edge.

Ketchum grumbled but forced himself to stir, letting his increased anger and pain fuel him. Getting up was a real struggle. He'd lost his cane and the AR-15 along the tumbling way as well as both pistols.

Without a light, he backtracked, gingerly taking wincing steps to where he'd first landed. He found the cane in the tops of the agarita bush. *Damn prickly thing. Typical Texas plant.* They should have all been pulled from the ground and burned years ago. He gave the bush a couple of hard whacks with his cane and nearly fell over with the effort.

The gun, being heavier, had tumbled a little farther away. He couldn't find the pistols and had no time to look more. He needed to be up the hill, after that bitch. When he had the AR-15 and the cane, he went over to the concrete path and steps that led to the house. That Quinn fellow would be busy up there for a spell. He might as well march right up the steps.

Ketchum's wounds throbbed, and he had to rub away a trickle of blood that came down from one eyebrow toward his eye. His body ached in several places.

If his mood hadn't already been pretty sour, he would have said it had gone up thirty degrees of mad from that. And that was pretty dog-gone blistering mad.

MAURY HAD BEEN STANDING in the front doorway, holding the shotgun and keeping an eye on the area in front of the house. They'd moved Fergie's car over to one side earlier so that he would have a clear view. When the shooting started, he dropped to the ground and slammed the door shut. Splinters flew as bullets passed through the front door, some slamming into the far wall and kitchen appliances. Tanner, who had been curled up in a corner, crouched even lower and stayed put.

Maury was sure glad they had sent Bonnie away with the baby in the boat. She would have been at one of the windows, firing back.

"You okay?" Al called out as he came in from the back and crawled to where Maury was crouched.

"Fine so far," Maury said. "But it's early times."

One of the front windows had been knocked out, spraying sparkling glass. Al took a look outside with the rifle's scope and squeezed off a shot toward where the flashes of gunfire were coming from.

The shooting paused then started again. Maybe he was just putting in a fresh clip.

"Any idea how many are out there?" Al asked, staying low.

"I can only count one, but I haven't been able to see out all that well since the shooting started."

"Could be a distraction. I'm gonna take a look out the back and fire a shot or two from the Glock to keep anyone from moving out there."

As he went through the house, he yanked out his phone. *Should have done that sooner.* He got an answering machine at Victor's house. Damned fool was probably already in bed, like normal people.

Next, he called the department and let the dispatcher know what was going on while taking a look out the back window. No one was out there that he could see, so he started back for the front of the house, where he went to the window, fired another shot at the flashes of gunfire, and dropped to the floor as more glass sprayed across him.

He glanced around. "You think my homeowner's insurance is going to buy that termites did this?"

"More like buzzing lead hornets," Maury said.

"Well, don't let any of them sting. Do like Tanner and stay low."

A couple more shots thudded into the front of the house, but the fusillade from out there wasn't as constant and crazy as it had been.

Maury opened the door a bit and fired a round from the Model 12 shotgun in that direction. When he saw an answering flash, he followed that with a couple of rounds from the Glock.

BONNIE SAT IN THE DRIVER'S seat of Al's fishing boat with Little Al in a papoose on her chest. She had tucked the boat into a side cove back a ways up Cow Creek, where Al had taken her and Maury to fish for bluegills and bass once while Fergie watched over the baby.

Back at the house, she had fired up the boat once the straps that held it up had lowered into the water, and she had drifted out into the lake. She remembered the direction Al took them and drove the boat at a slow, steady pace until she got to where she was anchored.

Fish rippled the surface around her as they came up to feed as the sky dimmed and grew gradually darker. A row of painted turtles were sunning on a log along the shore.

"Urdle. Urdle," Little Al said. But as the bow of the boat swung in the breeze, the turtles plopped off the log one by one and swam away underwater, only coming up now and then with a round little head to look around. Then they dipped below the surface and were gone again.

Waiting out on the lake by herself was maddening. She would have far preferred to be helping defend the house. It was her they wanted, after all. But the deciding aspect had been the little guy hanging on her chest. After a while, his eyes had closed, and his head pressed against her.

Something big splashed farther back around a bend in the creek, probably a big bass getting after something.

The night grew still, and the stars got brighter, until she felt she could nearly reach up and touch them, as short as she was.

Critters along the shore rustled among the dry leaves, while some birds in the trees moved about and made sounds she had heard when she hunted as a little girl with her pappy. One sounded like a distant cell phone ringing, but it wasn't one. She checked her phone, tempted to call and see how Maury was doing. He'd said he would call her when the coast was clear. *But what if he can't?* She had tried not to think about that.

In the peaceful night, she began to hear a distant popping, like grease in a pan. That was gunfire. The house was being attacked. But there was little she could do about that where she was. Bonnie had to sit and wait, though it nearly made her crazy. She had her Chiefs Special with her, but she couldn't use it just then. She had to sit and listen to the crackle of shots being exchanged, rifle shots along with the occasional deeper boom of the shotgun.

Sounds carried far too well across the water. Several times, she wanted to pull up the anchor and go back to the house as fast as she could. But staying was all about Little Al, not her. She made herself stay, though it ate at her not to know what was going on back there, whether Maury and Al were going to make it.

The sky and the lake around her had gotten dark. She was surrounded by splashes, the sounds of birds, and the wind rattling leafy limbs. After a while, Bonnie couldn't see a thing, but she could imagine all sorts. Her mind invented horrible details. She didn't like what she was thinking, but she couldn't stop. She clung to Little Al as tightly as she dared without waking him.

Far away, the popping crackle of gunfire continued while she could do nothing, nothing at all. That was the worst.

CABLE COULDN'T BELIEVE it. Of all of them, he was the one who'd come through so far without a wound. But he'd been hit and was bleeding. He fired a couple of rounds from the AR-15 and went back to wrapping the torn parts of his shirt around the wound on his upper left arm.

That damned rifle they used had done it. He should have done like he'd advised the others: move around when someone is using a scoped rifle. As simple as that. He tied the wrapping on his arm tightly, made a knot, and pulled it taut with his teeth. Then he went back to shooting at the house, but that time, he moved sideways a few feet as soon as he'd fired a few rounds.

Cable sure wished he had a grenade launcher. They'd obtained and lost some pretty effective gear without even getting to use most of it. Some of it had been dropped here and there. A good bit of it rested on the bottom of Lake Travis. All in all, the mission had been far from genius work by Ketchum.

And where the hell is Ketchum? He'd better not be trying to lead this battle from the far rear echelon. It was *his* fight, after all. He was the one who'd had the scrap-up with that curly-haired round blond bitch. He should be front and center, leading the charge. He was supposed to be attacking the Quinn place from the rear, but he was a no-show so far. Meanwhile, Buff was probably all cozy back at the trailer, knocking seven bells out of that tall, slender redhead and enjoying himself. *Damn. Life sure isn't fair.*

KETCHUM WAS MOVING slowly and hurting all the way, but he was nearing the back of the house, and at the moment, no one seemed to be guarding that side.

He could hear the fury of battle still happening on the other side of the house, but the shots didn't seem nearly as hot and heavy as before. He doubted Cable was getting bored, but something seemed to be the matter.

Ketchum got all the way to the back door without a challenge or shots fired at him. *Sweet.* He hoped that bitch was in there, just waiting for the justice of a bullet. The day so far had put him in a pretty foul mood, and he was mad. For him, the anger bar was always high, but at that moment, he wouldn't give a plugged nickel for her chances of surviving. Hell, he would kill all of them then light the house on fire and cut the hell out of there.

He reached to grasp the doorknob and damned if it wasn't locked. Ketchum tugged and twisted again but no luck.

After tucking his cane under one arm, he raised the AR-15 at the door's lock, but he stopped himself. Blasting in would announce his arrival and give those inside an opportunity to shoot him as he rushed inside. That wouldn't work and might just get him killed.

What a mess! He started around the house toward the front, doubting that anyone would be looking out the side windows. Clinging to the shadow that ran along the base of the house, he was achy and sore from falling off the small cliff, so he took longer than he would have liked. But soon, he was nearly all the way up the sloping hill and almost to the front corner of the house.

Cable's AR-15 was still barking away. *Good.* As close as he was to the front door, Ketchum had to stop and take deep breaths, reaching down to rub his leg. The tumble down the hill had done quite a bit of no good to his already-hurt leg. If he hadn't found his cane again, he would probably still be down there in the stickers, thrashing around like a turtle on its back.

As it was, he felt used up and out of steam. But he stood as straight as he could and shook himself. He had only a little farther to go. *Then I'll have all this behind me. Suck it up and keep going,* he told himself. He cradled his AR-15 with one hand and pushed at the ground with his cane. Ketchum had just a little farther to go to round the corner at the front of the house.

FERGIE'S LONG LEGS churned away, eating up the distance, but they seemed to be slowing down. She couldn't imagine why. Her ankle hurt from where it had been chafed raw by the chain. *Slavery.* That was the tone they'd been seeking to set, and fear, with an inevitable bullet at the end of it all. All because one of them had gotten into a tiff on a highway.

The worst thing about overgrown children like that was they thought they were right, that being enraged was a natural response in a situation like that.

The sky and woods around her, even the gates of the lanes she passed, were all dark. The smell in the air was of rotting, mildly moist woods, leaves, and dirt.

She still clung to the stupid softball bat, swinging it beside her with each step like a relay-race baton. It made her feel like a member of a team that worked together. That made her wonder for just part of a second if they'd ever be the same happy family out by the lake after all they had gone through. She guessed she would have to wait and see.

Finally, she came to the end of Al's lane. Hell, it was *their* lane—hers and the rest of them. She had been rattled. She admitted that. But she was going home.

The lane was mostly gravel. *Great.* Her feet were sore, and she was pretty sure she'd worn most of the bottoms of her socks away and was running barefoot and maybe bleeding a little. But she didn't have that much farther to go.

Gunfire sounded ahead. So it had started. She could have no idea how it was going, but she wanted to be there, to be a part of it and defend her home. Fergie started to run even faster, though each step hurt to the core of her being.

Chapter Twenty-Eight

That Al guy came scrambling out the door with a rifle, like a rat deserting a sinking ship. But instead of running off, he took up a new position behind a tree to fire a shot at Cable. Maybe he was finally taking exception to having his house turned into Swiss cheese. *Well, good.* The pot had needed stirring. Now the guy seemed riled himself and just needed to get closer to Cable so Cable could take him down.

But that didn't seem to be Al's plan. Each time he fired a shot at Cable, it came from a different place. He was hopping around like some kind of Mexican bean.

Cable fired several rounds into a twitching mountain laurel bush, yet the return fire came from twenty feet away in a new spot. *He wants to play games, does he?*

Cable's arm was wounded, but his feet and legs were okay. He sprang to his feet and ran in a zigzag toward the house's front door.

The rifle in the woods sounded, but the shot missed him. The front door opened, and a shotgun blast came from there. He felt it hard, nearly impossible, to cover both shooters at the same time. But he had to do it somehow. *Where the hell is Ketchum?*

Swinging the AR-15, Cable ran toward the front door. He zigged and zagged, firing the whole way. The shotgun sounded again, and he felt a blaze of heat in his right knee. Then all he felt was fire in his leg. He dropped the assault rifle and grabbed at his knee, falling to the ground.

Cable tried to rise but couldn't. His knee was hamburger. That damn fool had gotten him. Cable knew better too. Unlike a rifle with a scope, movement wasn't foolproof against a shotgun. Someone could always lead you a bit, and a shotgun blast covered more space.

Cable was still holding his knee when he heard footsteps running toward him—that Al guy with the rifle. He grabbed for the Colt .45 in his belt, but as he was raising the gun, Al kicked his hand and sent the handgun flying. When Cable went for his belt knife, Al grabbed and twisted that arm until it cracked.

Cable followed Al's glance toward the door. The other guy lay on the ground, halfway out it. *Good.* He'd at least gotten one of them. While Al was looking away, Cable tried to crawl to where the AR-15 had fallen. Al spun, saw him moving, and rushed forward to stomp on Cable's extended hand.

As best as he could, Cable crawled toward where the pistol and rifle lay. He thought Al was going to rush in and hurt him again. But Al showed a strong will and made himself stop. He might well be angry—an infectious anger in the heat of a fight, which Cable knew well—but he could see Al resist it. Instead, he moved faster than Cable could and got to the weapons first. Al grabbed the rifle, pistol, and knife and threw them as far away as he could. Then he took off in a run toward the house.

WHEN AL GOT TO THE door, he saw blood on Maury's shirt and turned him over. His brother was unconscious, probably from the shock of getting hit with a bullet. He tore off Maury's shirt. It looked like the bullet had passed through Maury's side. Al didn't think it had hit any organs. But a steady flow of blood seeped from the entrance and exit wounds. That had to be stopped right then, or Maury would bleed out.

Al rushed to the kitchen, which was in shambles, and grabbed a stack of towels and a bowl he filled with water. At least the faucet worked, although it looked like the stove and fridge would never function again. He carried the water and towels over and got down beside Maury. He wished Bonnie were there. As a trained nurse, she would know what to do.

But Al had no time for wishing. He cleaned the wound openings and began to press towels to them. Soon, they turned pink.

KETCHUM EASED AROUND the front corner of the house just in time to see a pair of legs being pulled into the house. Well, someone was down. *Good.*

He was about to slip over to the door and see if he could catch them by surprise when he saw Cable on the ground halfway to the house.

Ketchum ducked low and scurried over to where Cable sat on his haunches with his arms around his shins. Blood was oozing from one knee, and a trickle of it ran down his right cheek from his closed eye, where he must have caught at least one of the shotgun pellets.

As Ketchum got closer, he could see one arm was broken.

"You're a right mess, Cable."

"Can't argue with you 'bout that. That Quinn fella done all this to me. Can you give me a hand gettin' outta here?"

"Your knee's a mess, and the same goes for your arm and hand."

"They hurt quite a bit. Can you help me up?"

"Really? You're letting me down, Cable." He glanced at the house.

"Where were you while I was getting the worst of it?"

"Are you questioning my authority?"

"You have no authority, Ketchum. You hate authority. Always have."

Ketchum shook his head. "*Tsk. Tsk.* Cable, this ain't shapin' up to be a very good day for you."

"What're you sayin'?"

"I'm saying bye, old pard."

"You can't mean—"

"Oh, but I do."

Cable scrambled to crawl away, as crippled as he was. Just as he was about to claw his way to where his AR-15 and Colt .45 lay, Ketchum limped there faster and stepped on Cable's extended hand. He heard and felt what seemed like every bone in it crumble. Cable raised the hand, and the fingers dangled loose.

"Well, well, Cable. It's Kentucky Derby day, and you've fallen at Churchill Downs and have a broken leg. You know what happens next."

Cable looked up at Ketchum, his eyes pleading and mad at the same time. But the pleading was not enough.

Ketchum pointed the barrel of his AR-15 at Cable's forehead and squeezed off a single shot.

He turned toward the house, expecting someone to have noticed. The door was slightly ajar, but he couldn't see anyone. He moved slowly that way, tired to every single bone but determined to do what he'd come to do.

As he got closer, he could see one of them on the floor, the other bent over him, pressing towels over wounds exposed by the torn-away shirt.

Ketchum gave a tired, grim grin. It was going to feel so good to get all this wrapped up at last.

Chapter Twenty-Nine

Al was pressing towels against Maury's wounds when he heard a sound from the doorway. He knew he needed to defend the house, but the bleeding had to be stopped, or he would lose Maury, whose face was already paler. He looked up toward the sound.

Ketchum stood there, holding himself upright with a cane while with the other hand he was pointing his AR-15 at Al.

Al had just been thinking back over the twenty years when he hadn't spoken to Maury. Then, Al had lived apart from everyone, just doing his job and fishing some. He'd thought something was wrong with him, but Fergie, Maury, Bonnie, and even Tanner had helped fix that. He had come to know something bigger too. Love wasn't about getting. It was about giving.

The asshole standing behind him threatened all that. He was the kind of jerk who got mad for reasons that should have affected no other person, and he had been like a tornado spinning out of control through their lives, all because of his uncontrollable and unmanageable anger.

"You made a right mess out of Cable out there," Ketchum said.

"He brought it on himself."

Ketchum rocked back a half step and nearly fired. But he had an agenda first. "Where's the bitch who shot me?"

So it's going to be like that. Al shook his head and kept pressing on Maury's wounds. The lug nut standing over them was going to have to rant before pulling the trigger, going on about how satisfying it was going to be, his revenge, his payback.

"Where?" Ketchum shouted. "Tell me where!"

In the corner of Al's eye, Tanner slowly got to his feet, as old and wounded as he was. He charged Ketchum in a white-wrapped blur. Maybe he remembered that Ketchum was the one who'd shot him through the door. Or perhaps he just sensed that he was a very bad man who was threatening the family.

Tanner's leap surprised Ketchum and knocked the rifle from his hand and nearly knocked him over.

Ketchum struggled with the dog while reaching to get his gun back. He was just raising the AR-15 once again when Fergie came in the front door. She stood there in her stocking feet, carrying an aluminum softball bat.

"Where's that bitch?" Ketchum yelled.

Tanner moved in and got a grip on his jeans leg and started pulling, nearly getting him off balance.

"Right behind you," Fergie said.

Ketchum's eyes opened wide, and he started to turn toward her. His head was ahead of his gun barrel as he turned. He saw Fergie, his eyes popping still wider, and had to look up just as she swung the bat toward the other side of his head and hit it on the temple with a hollow gong sound.

"At the sound of the chime," she said as he crumpled, "it'll be time for your nap."

His rifle clattered to the floor as he fell forward across it, his cheek pressing down as the bulk of his body followed with a thud. Tanner didn't let go of his leg but kept tugging.

"Quick. Give me a hand with Maury," Al said. "I owe you a thousand hugs later. I'm so glad to see you alive. I thought..."

She gave him an affectionate shove and bent over Maury.

"There's another of them out there," Al said. "I only wounded him. He's still alive and prone to be scrappy."

"No, he's not alive. Ketchum saw to that. Shot his own sidekick dead. I watched him do it. I was coming down the lane and caught the whole thing. It's a good thing he didn't look my way, or he might've shot me too."

Fergie took over pressing the towels against Maury. Before Al dashed to get gauze and tape, he quickly checked Tanner. The dog was okay and possibly quietly proud, if the tail wag meant anything.

Then Al put his arms around Fergie and looked into her eyes. "I thought you might be dead."

"I didn't have a fun time, but I managed to get clear of there in the end. After the way they treated and threatened me, I should have swung for the cheap seats. But that would have made me as rotten as they are. Anyway, Clayton wants them alive, so let's wrap this one up with duct tape and put a bow on him."

As he rushed back with their first aid kit, Al said, "You're sure about the one on the front lawn? He was alive when I left him."

"I'm sure. But that was none of my doing. Don't touch Ketchum's rifle. His prints'll still be on it. It's a murder weapon now."

In the distance, the sounds of sirens were headed their way.

Al got on the phone to the department again. "We're going to need an ambulance, too, and a coroner. There are two wounded here and one beyond caring, but I want to make it very clear that my brother, Maury, gets treated first."

The dispatcher replied, "I hear you on that, loud and clear, and I'll pass it along."

Chapter Thirty

Bonnie came around the corner into the living room, still puffing after climbing up the steps from downstairs. "Finally got the little fellow to sleep. Did I miss anything? After waiting all these months, I wouldn't want to miss how the trial ended."

"I don't think any of us made it into the news coverage, which is just as well," Fergie said. "All we did was confirm what we said in our statements. But they did show the footage of the original road rage incident, and when you got out of the truck and started to shoot back at Ketchum, some people in the courtroom cheered. The judge had to shush them."

Bonnie shook her head but grinned in spite of herself. She went over to stand beside Maury, who sat in one of the chairs at the new kitchen table they'd gotten from the Amish furniture company. She ran a hand across the wood, which was so smooth and polished that it felt like silk.

Maury put an arm around her waist and pulled her close. He had to sit in a straight chair to get up and down. His chest was still wrapped, though he was already moving about a lot better. Still, the nurse in Bonnie kind of enjoyed giving him a little of the ol' TLC.

A fire was going in the fireplace, since a touch of chill in the air merited it, and Al had added just enough mesquite to the oak to fill the house with its embracing smell.

Al and Fergie sat on the new leather couch with a bowl of popcorn between them. They all looked toward the big-screen television, where a news anchor was just rehashing the result of Ketchum's trial. One of the forensic crew was testifying.

"I'm glad we avoided as much as we could of all that," Fergie said, "except when we had to testify ourselves, with Ketchum glaring at us and yelling, 'Lies!' until they had to remove him until we were done."

The prosecution team had a ton of forensic evidence, but when they told Kale how Ketchum had killed Cable, Kale got the shakes, and they got a big boost when he took a plea bargain and ratted the rest of them out, singing like the entire Mormon Tabernacle Choir. So they solved a lot of the murders, vehicle thefts, and the rest all in one swoop. Victor said a key point in the plea bargain was that Kale would be kept away from Ketchum in prison, and so would Biff and Buff. He described Buff snapping the guy's neck at the armory in great detail.

"As far as I could tell, Ketchum was one of those loyalty-is-a-one-way-street guys," Fergie said. "That especially goes for that Cable guy, who I saw Ketchum shoot down like a dog. Oh, sorry, Tanner."

"Oh, here comes the part Victor told me about." Al nodded toward the television. "I thought they'd show this."

"I do enjoy the big screen," Bonnie said. "We're gonna have to watch some movies together on this thing."

The clip on the TV started just as Ketchum interrupted Kale's testimony by leaping to his feet and yelling, "I'll kill you, you rat fink sonuvabitch!"

The court-appointed defense lawyer lowered his head into his hands.

Bonnie shook her head at the pandemonium of Ketchum being dragged from the courtroom while flailing his arms about, kicking, and yelling as loudly as he could. "Oh, my oh my. I wish I'd been there in the courtroom to see that."

"That was the third and last time he was removed from the courtroom," Fergie said. "But I doubt contempt of court is going to weigh much among the other charges of murder, kidnapping, criminal trespassing, and vehicle theft."

Once the news anchor announced the guilty-on-all-counts verdict, he moved on to another story.

Al reached for the remote and flipped off the television. "I hope this new big screen isn't going to keep us from getting outdoors as much as we can and enjoying life."

"Don't forget all these other new wonders." Bonnie waved a hand toward the range and fridge. "That thing makes ice and cold water. It's one heck of a way to get new things, but by gosh, they're nice to have. Now we just have the outside of the house to finish with a paint job tomorrow, and we're gonna be as sparkly new as a freshly dropped spotted fawn. That wackjob Ketchum did us a roundabout favor."

"If you put aside his kidnapping Fergie and damn well trying to kill the rest of us." Maury patted where he still had bandages under his shirt. "It wasn't all a stroll in the park, and if given the chance to do it all again, I'd pass."

"I'm sure Fergie could do without being kidnapped and wondering from one minute to the next if she was going to live through it," Al said.

"Admit it." Fergie gave his shoulder a gentle shove. "You were sweating that part too."

"I damn well was. After finally letting down my guard after all these years, I couldn't begin to imagine how I was going to live without you."

She moved the popcorn and slid across the couch to sit closer. "Well, let's just savor every second from now on."

Chapter Thirty-One

Clayton drove down the lane to Al's place in his Lincoln Town Car and slowed when he got to all manner of vehicles parked in a cluster near the house. He wore old clothes, since Bess had warned him it was a house-painting day when she said he could come. In fact, she had insisted on it. She thought of Al Quinn as a son too. Clayton had on worn blue coveralls he didn't even know he still owned—Bess had found them somewhere among his things—over a red-checked flannel shirt that made him feel slightly like Father Christmas.

He parked behind a truck that belonged to Victor Kahlon and pulled his jacket tighter around him against the chill of a mid-December day that was trying to ease toward Texas's idea of a brief winter.

The front of the house was on its way to looking as good as it ever had, almost new and certainly better than when it had been peppered by bullet holes and the broken windows had been turned into sparkles of shattered glass across the ground.

People were all over the place, some on ladders and some at ground level as they wielded paint brushes and rollers. He knew them all. There was Dirty Fingernails Huff, with a possum tucked into a baby papoose on his chest. Both were spattered with sky-blue paint.

Meat Jenkins wore blue coveralls much like Clayton's. He carried a bucket of paint over to pour into a tray where Al was dipping a roller. Fergie was up on a ladder, touching up the trim with white paint where the blue on the siding had already dried.

Deputies Bob and Sandel were painting away, and Victor had a big smear of blue paint across one cheek as he touched up the area around the front door.

"Someone get me a brush," Clayton said. "I'm no Van Gogh, but I'll do what I can. I'm glad to see the rest of you lot out here helping out."

He looked around at each of them, knowing he probably had a twinkle in his eyes. Through the years, Al Quinn had become something like an ersatz son to him, and he'd come to think of the whole houseful of them as family. He probably wouldn't admit to that if asked, but he was ready to chip in with a little work himself.

Bonnie handed him a wide natural-bristle paint brush. "Glad to see you joining in. We should have this sucker done by sunset with you all helping out." Paint was speckled across her forehead and the front of her bobbing curly blond hair. She went back to work on a lower level of the white trim.

"You didn't have to come out and pitch in to help personally," Al said.

"Least I can do," Clayton said, "since y'all did your part in kicking off our countywide campaign against road rage. You helped me with my agenda. I can damn well help you with yours."

He nodded to Maury, who sat at a picnic table covered with a red-and-white-checked plastic tablecloth that held a metal tub of long-necked beers, which no one had touched yet, as well as pies, cake, and bowls of fruit, potato salad, and slaw. The slice or two missing from an apple pie suggested Meat Jenkins had tried a small sample.

Maury had Little Al on his lap and was letting him grab pieces of fruit out of a bowl with his fingers.

"More," Little Al said as he raised a piece of pear toward his mouth.

Maury's oversize flannel shirt covered the bandages he still wore over his almost-healed wounds.

"You feeling a good spell better?" Clayton asked him.

"Getting shot while in my sixties has been no joke. But having to chase a much-younger wife around is the best rehab I could ask for. She keeps me motivated."

"I hear the inside of the place looks great too," Clayton said to change the subject as he moved between Al and Bonnie to start painting away.

"All thanks to you and the others from the department," Bonnie said. "I'm loving our new fridge and range."

"She wants to cook all the time," Maury said. "It's a wonder we aren't all perfectly round."

"Some of us are." Bonnie grinned.

"The homeowner's-insurance adjuster said they wouldn't pay if it had been one bullet hitting the house," Fergie said. "When he visited, he looked around with an open mouth, and on his clipboard, he wrote, 'More than one bullet.' But these off-duty deputies and you coming out to help are the biggest real blessing to get us back to so-called normal."

Clayton grinned. "That's because you guys are a bit of folklore at the department by now, especially including Bonnie's shooting skills. Tanner too." He glanced over at the dog, who had moved close to press against Maury's leg. His wrappings were off, and his fur had nearly grown back.

"That Ketchum fellow was the one who talked about getting payback," Bonnie said, "but it was Tanner who got that in the end."

"The guys keep asking if Fergie wants to come play on the department's mixed softball team, the way she handled that Buff fellow and Ketchum."

"I still have the bat," she said, "for happy memories... and home defense."

"And I'm grateful that Bonnie made it through all this without punching someone's ticket for good with that little gun of hers." Clayton shook his head. "The only casualty those guys had in that department turned into one more strike against Ketchum, with some of the hardest evidence we had."

"If you think being on a boat at night with Little Al while hearing gunfire in the distance was a joy, then you'd be wrong. I wanted to be here, defending our home."

"You won't have to defend against any of those guys," Victor said. "They'll all be in prison for the rest of your lifetimes."

Al gave Clayton a grin. "You were a real hoot at Ketchum's trial. You said you didn't want a trial by media, but I hear you dropped the phrase 'road rage' a dozen times during your testimony."

The corner of Clayton's mouth tugged up. His agenda to put road rage in the spotlight had been quite clear, and the media had gobbled it up like biscuits and gravy.

"Happy times," Fergie said, "which we're so pleased to leave behind us."

"Amen to that." Clayton raised his paint brush in a salute. "By the way, one thing I especially came out here to tell you about was that Ketchum had one of those fall-down-the-stairs accidents. Actually, he got beat down to the ground by other inmates on his first day inside. The way I heard it was he went up to a couple of the biggest dudes he could find and asked something like "Which of you girls wants to be my bodyguard?" When someone explained that meant trading sexual favors, that lit his fuse, and he started the fight. Prison is sure no place to go to with a mad on. I heard he lost several teeth and almost an eye, so then he really had something to be angry about."

"It's a funny thing, and I can't explain it," Bonnie said. "But his anger and hate has somehow made all of us more peaceful and understanding."

"I wish I could say that my efforts and what you folks have been through along with the media's coverage would make a difference," Clayton said. "But in a gradually more overcrowded world where some people are always stirring one another up, I don't know that we can count on that."

"That's a lofty wish," Al said, "but I'm coming to think we can't fix others. We can only really work on ourselves."

"And Lord knows, we all need it," Bonnie said.

Clayton just nodded, smiled, and kept painting.

About the Author

Russ Hall lives on the north shore of Lake Travis near Austin, TX. An award-winning writer of mysteries, thrillers, westerns, poetry, and nonfiction books, he has had more than thirty-five books published, as well as numerous short stories and articles. He has also been on *The New York Times* bestseller list multiple times with co-authored nonfiction books, such as: *Do You Matter: How Great Design Will Make People Love Your Company* (Financial Times Press, 2009) with Richard Brunner, former head of design at Apple, and *Identity* (Financial Times Press, 2012) with Stedman Graham, Oprah's companion.

He was an editor for over 35 years with major publishing companies, ranging from Harper & Row (now HarperCollins) to Simon & Schuster to Pearson. He has been a pet rescue center volunteer, a mountain climber, and a probable book hoarder who fishes and hikes in his spare moments.

Read more at www.russhall.com.

About the Publisher

Dear Reader,

We hope you enjoyed this book. Please consider leaving a review on your favorite book site.

Visit https://RedAdeptPublishing.com to see our entire catalogue.

Check out our app for short stories, articles, and interviews. You'll also be notified of future releases and special sales.